THE GAME ON
THATCHER
ISLAND

THE GAME ON THATCHER ISLAND

T. DEGENS

THE VIKING PRESS
NEW YORK

First Edition
Copyright © T. Degens, 1977
All rights reserved
First published in 1977 by The Viking Press
625 Madison Avenue, New York, N.Y. 10022
Published simultaneously in Canada by
Penguin Books Canada Limited
Printed in U.S.A.
1 2 3 4 5 81 80 79 78 77

Library of Congress Cataloging in Publication Data
Degens, T. The game on Thatcher Island.
Summary: Harry is flattered when a group of older boys invite
him to join their game on Thatcher Island, but his elation
disappears when he realizes their game is one of terror.
I. Title.
PZ7.D3637Gam   [Fic]   77-24166
ISBN 0-670-33393-X

THE GAME ON
THATCHER
ISLAND

PART
I

Just outside the harbor of a small New England town, Thatcher Island, with its colorful history, is an appealing and even provocative hideaway for picnickers; and when the Morrison boys ask Harry to join them for a secret "war game" on Thatcher Island, eleven-year-old Harry is intensely flattered. But there are problems: his younger sister Sarah, for one; the Fresh Air Fund boy, John, for another. John would be arriving that very week, and Sarah had found out about the "picnic." Harry decides to take them along—they could help. Before he realizes what has happened or why, Harry has "borrowed" his father's whaler and is anchored offshore, the beach of Thatcher Island within easy reach. Then the game begins, and Harry is shocked to learn that in this war game he, Sarah, and John are the enemy.

In this gripping novel, T. Degens writes sympathetically about a boy whose innocent vanity and weakness lead him to the terrible moment when he discovers for the first time that he is capable of cruelty.

The island was three miles long and a mile wide, more or less. It floated in the ocean not far from the entrance to Salt Meadow Bay like an enormous seal, its head lifted above the water as if guarding against surprise.

Harry had noticed them too late. The group of boys filled the narrow passage between the cars, blocking his way back from the ice cream truck and across the Quamhassett Beach parking lot to the water. He was too close now to steer another course, to shift in a wide turn toward the northern exit without attracting special attention. Nervously he licked the ice cream down to its still hard frozen core, pausing to brace himself. Then he walked on, straight ahead.

"What's your hurry, Chase?" It was Patrick Morrison, towering two heads above Harry.

"Nothing," mumbled Harry, taking another step between the dark red VW bus and the blue Dodge station wagon, both with their doors open. A leg bridged the gap. Harry stopped. It was a big, powerful, tanned and hairy leg that belonged to Gordon Schwendiman, who leaned back in the rear seat of the Dodge, grinning up at Harry.

"You want to be on our team in a game of war?" Patrick's brother Doug addressed him, squatting on the hood.

Harry was so stunned that he could only nod.

"Saturday on Thatcher Island. We might even stay overnight. Haven't had a hunt in the dark for a long time," said Doug.

"Hunt him?" asked Gordon Schwendiman lazily, pointing his toes toward Harry. The big one was blue and the nail was splintered.

"He'd be quick enough. Wouldn't you, Chase?" Rhino came up from behind, jabbing his finger into Harry's back. He was the massive defensive tackle of the school football team.

Harry nodded again while the ice cream ran down his hand, along the skin of his arm, and dripped off his elbow. There was laughter and he laughed with them.

"He's only kidding," said Doug. "We need you, Chase. Messages, you know. Scouting. General squirrel work. You'll be great." It did not sound like a question, it sounded like a statement, and Harry raised his head, hot with pleasure.

"That's arranged then. Thatcher Island on Saturday! Bring your own supplies. We'll get in touch about details." Doug slid off the hood. "And not a word to anybody!"

"Not a word," repeated Gordon Schwendiman, still amused.

"What a mess!" Rhino knocked the ice cream cone out of Harry's hand as he crammed his huge hard chest and belly past him. "Sticky, eh?" They walked off and left him splattered, burning his bare feet on the hot asphalt, overwhelmed with feeling proud and important and terribly flattered. Flattered that Doug and Patrick Morrison had asked *him*, Harry Wheeler Chase, who was only in the sixth grade and whom they had hardly talked to before, to join their game.

"We need you, Chase," Doug had said, and with those words his earlier qualms had been wiped away.

Harry looked after them, speechless. "Yes," he wanted to shout. "I'll be there. You can count on me. I'll be there!"

He saw himself in the center of the school yard with kids crowding around, eager to listen to him tell about his day with Doug and Patrick and the other tenth graders on the island. For once they were going to crowd around him and not Wesley or Bruce Delaney.

"Harry, Harry!"

He breathed in deeply. The skin tingled where the

(3)

ice cream was drying. The cone had been knocked out of his hand by accident. It hadn't been Rhino's fault. Had it?

Doug and Patrick must have picked him because of his scouting awards, Harry thought. He had won two just last week, one in tracking and the other in basket weaving. There had been a picture of him in the local paper, examining the blurred ground, with the caption: "Winner reads bear wolf squirrel correctly." What luck they had not taken a shot of him and the basket! And what luck he hadn't had time to duck behind a car and sneak off after he had recognized Doug Morrison and remembered what had occurred three weeks ago on the bus. Though he had expected Doug to tell the others about it. And laugh.

Two stops down the road on the last day of school Doug had slumped into the seat next to him. Harry had been thrilled listening to Doug's banter with a couple of girls across the aisle. Suddenly he had felt something cold and sharp relentlessly pressing down on his throat. A knife! For an awful moment he had imagined his throat being cut, the throbbing pain, the blood gurgling, a flap of skin hanging down. He had waited, trembling hands folded, without the slightest movement. Abruptly the pressure had stopped. Doug had waved his metal comb in front of Harry's eyes and went on combing his thick brown hair while one of the girls giggled and Harry sat stiffly, too humiliated to say anything. He

(4)

should have pushed Doug's arm away. He knew all the time it wasn't a knife.

And now what incredible luck.

Running to the water to wash and cool his feet he thought of the kid from New York City. He was not going to let him spoil the game. He would simply ask his parents to have him come a week later.

"Where's the ice cream?" asked Sarah when he caught up with her.

Harry shrugged his shoulders. "Melted, I guess."

"All of it? What took you so long?"

"I met some kids," explained Harry, and then he went on, because he had to tell someone and Sarah wasn't anybody but his sister and could be relied on to keep a secret and at the same time look up to him with respect. "The Morrisons asked me to be on their team for a game on Thatcher Island this Saturday!"

"Thatcher Island, that's my most favorite island," cried Sarah, neglecting all the other information.

"You hardly even know it," said Harry, rather disappointed that she got excited about the least important point. "We always go to Forbes Island."

"It's still my most favorite island. I'll come too!"

"You aren't invited." Harry had to be blunt. "Besides, it's overnight. You must be crazy if you think mother and dad will let you go."

"We'll tell them it's a picnic. And we don't have to stay overnight. I wouldn't mind." Sarah beamed at him.

"Take you along?" cried Harry. "Never!"

"I don't even want to be in the game," Sarah went on, unperturbed. "Stupid game! I won't bother anybody. Promise!"

"Like at my last birthday party when you won every single prize because you had found the answers to the riddles on mother's desk?"

"That was different," declared Sarah. "I needed the prizes. And I left you alone when I got them, didn't I?"

"You needed them," sneered Harry. "What for, that's what I'd like to know! Why would you need six Indian tomahawks? Never mind." She probably didn't remember what had been so urgent about the tomahawks. Something to do with her dolls.

Sarah was about to open her mouth, but closed it and after a moment went back to the main subject. "Harry, listen! Why don't you bring me along as a surprise. Like you had to take me with you at the last second."

"Some surprise!" He should have kept his mouth shut. How was he to know Sarah cared that much about Thatcher Island? She had never mentioned it before. Still, he regarded her thoughtfully. He might have to use her idea of the picnic to get permission to go.

"I'll think about it," Harry said. "But it's top secret till I give the sign." Sarah nodded solemnly.

They went for their bikes and pedaled out on the road and turned right in the direction of their house. Sarah rode in silence to let Harry think. She didn't even get furious when Harry crashed into her back wheel. Thinking usually takes a lot of your attention.

Harry pedaled blindly. Different pictures kept flashing through his mind. Glorious pictures. Harry crawling through the underbrush and discovering the enemy hideout. Harry taking three prisoners singlehanded. Harry commended in front of the others. Harry walking in the school yard with Doug and Patrick, Gordon, Rhino, and the other tenth graders. Not like Bruce Delaney or Wesley, who were tolerated at the fringes and sent on errands.

"Get me a Coke, Bruce!" And Bruce would run, happy.

"This towel is wet, Wes!" And Wesley would supply a dry one.

He could hear Doug say, "Get a Coke for Harry!" and see Bruce and Wesley both rush away.

Harry pedaled faster and began to whistle.

———————

The island was an ordinary northern island, like a hundred others, windswept, bleached, the beaches littered with whatever the waves carried ashore. Its coast was rocky and sandy in turn, steep toward the open sea, rising seventy-five feet above the water at Gull's Head and stretching flat and desolate to Baker's Point across from the mainland. The thin soil supported scrub oaks, cedars and pines, sumac,

(7)

birches, a few maples, various briers and weeds,
berry bushes, beach grasses, creeping roses, honey-
suckle, poison ivy, wild flowers. And grapevines.

"When is he coming?" asked Harry, and he was
pleased that his voice sounded so casual. His family did
not seem to hear him. Mrs. Chase turned to the local
page in her newspaper; Sarah was absorbed in coloring
her puffed wheat pink with raspberry jam. His father
went on searching for his car keys as he did nearly every
morning, rummaging in the kitchen drawers among old
bills, ice cream sticks, broken shoe laces, rubber bands,
grocery coupons.

"On the piano," said his mother without looking up.
"Your keys are on the piano. What did you say, Harry?"

Harry watched his father leave the kitchen and reach
for the keys on the piano in the living room, drop them
in his pocket, straighten his tie, mutter some words in
their direction, pull his tie loose, and walk out of sight
toward the front door. When the door closed, he
blinked his eyes and turned back to his mother.

"The Fresh Air kid. The boy from New York. When
does he come?"

"Today is Monday. It must be on Thursday. Yes,
I'm sure Thursday." Mrs. Chase read on.

"Let him come a week later," demanded Harry, and
this time he did not hide his interest. Instantly Sarah
switched her attention to him, and a spoonful of jam
dripped on the table.

(8)

"But Harry, you knew all along he would be coming this week!" exclaimed his mother. "We don't set the date. That's done by the Fresh Air Fund in New York City. They're sending kids to Egham twice this summer."

"Couldn't he come with the second batch?" Harry snapped. He was angry because he simply had not anticipated any difficulties. If they were inviting somebody they didn't even know, couldn't they at least set the date as they pleased?

"Harry, what's got into you?" Mrs. Chase put her paper down and studied Harry, who in turn studied the familiar pattern of the wallpaper above her head. Always the same yellow geometrical lines that divided the dark red into diamonds.

"Nothing," he said as calmly as he could to the wall. Then he forced a smile and looked directly at his mother. "I didn't mean anything special." But it was too late.

"Don't you want him to come?" Mrs. Chase looked and sounded hurt.

"Harry didn't say anything like that," cried Sarah.

"I didn't mean anything," insisted Harry. But he could not keep his voice down.

Mrs. Chase ignored Sarah.

"Don't shout, Harry," she said. "Don't you remember we talked it over and we all agreed to share our summer with someone not as fortunate as we are?"

Harry groaned. Nothing was going to stop her now.

Mrs. Chase went on in a tone of utter reasonableness to remind them of their discussion some time ago in the spring when they had decided to invite a Fresh Air child for the summer. It was the voice she always adopted when Harry and Sarah were supposed to make up their own minds, while all the good arguments were on her side and opposing them meant you were either bad or stupid. Like choosing the apple and not the candy bar for dessert. Or coming along for a Sunday afternoon visit to the Rest Haven Nursing Home, where grandmother had to live, instead of hanging around at home with nothing really urgent to do. Harry stared at the wallpaper again. He couldn't tell her about the Morrisons and Thatcher Island. She wouldn't understand the importance of being asked to join the game. Besides, he wasn't allowed to talk about it. But why did she have to repeat all that? Go on and on?

Sarah rubbed the raspberry jam into a gooey circle on the table, eyes half closed, the three middle fingers going round and round, shielded from her mother's voice. They did remember the evening and at least some of the arguments in favor of inviting a Fresh Air child.

It is hot in New York.

It is crowded.

One can hardly breathe because of air pollution.

There is no place to play but the streets.

The streets are dirty and dangerous.

Sometimes the garbage isn't picked up for weeks and weeks.

People are poor; they don't have money to go to the beach or a pool.

They don't have money for air conditioning.

Harry does have an extra bed in his room.

We are certainly not rich but we are quite comfortable.

There are beaches all around us.

It will be an experience for all of us.

The arguments nobody spoke aloud, Harry thought, went like this:

It's awful.

I'll be stuck with him all summer and I don't even know him.

Maybe he is one of the kids nobody can stand. Like Fraser, who never washes himself and stinks something terrible.

Or Cunningham, who trips people and pulls chairs away from under you.

Or Susan Shanowsky, who bullies everybody.

What do I do if I hate him?

Then Harry had said he wouldn't mind, after he learned that "sharing your summer" translated into a two-week visit and not one day more. Which they should have explained in the beginning. He knew he would have to share his room, with his books and models, his race-car track and record player, his stamp collection and his comics. And his time. In fact, he decided, most of the "sharing," if not all, was going to be done by him.

"That's my boy." His father had kneaded his shoulder and Harry had noted the satisfied expression on his mother's face. He would be free after two weeks with a lot of credit for having done the right thing. Moreover, he really didn't mind having another kid around for such a short time.

Sarah had said the stranger wasn't going to be allowed to touch the dishes and the painted grandfather clock from Bavaria and the tiny lamps which actually lit up in her doll's house. When Mr. Chase had told her not to be small-minded, she had declared he could not touch her bike either. But since Sarah was only eight, her father and mother had laughed and let it pass.

That had been months ago.

"So I am sure we will all have a very good time together," ended Mrs. Chase, and smiled at Harry and Sarah. "Now run along to the beach. You shouldn't be late for your swimming lessons."

Sarah ran after Harry and caught up with him on the way to the shed to pick up their bikes.

"It doesn't matter if you bring one along or two," she said. "I'll take care of the Fresh Air kid as long as you want me to. We'll go on a treasure hunt."

Harry grunted.

"They'll let us go, all three of us, for a picnic on Thatcher Island!"

"Why don't you leave me alone?" barked Harry. "And I don't feel like swimming lessons. I'm going to the dunes."

Angry, he rode out on the road. Sarah was right, of course. It would be a cinch to get permission for all three of them to go on a picnic with friends. But the moment he appeared at the dock with Sarah and the strange kid, he was sure to be kicked out of the game.

"It's a game of war, Chase."

"We aren't fighting babies."

It was a game of war, after all, where he would have to prove himself.

"Messages, scouting," Doug had said, and Harry wondered what else was required of him. He had to know more about the game.

Harry took a left turn and a second left after he passed the huge elm tree. The narrow road was fenced in by stone walls; meadows stretched to distant woods beyond. Farther along, the trees came up to the road, low scraggly trees, pines and oaks with vines creeping over them. A border of cattails separated the woods from the marsh, a different kind of meadow, low and dark green, crisscrossed by streams and channels and ditches. Moist dark mud glistened on the walls of the waterways.

He pedaled along the marsh. Now the other side of the road was lined with houses, shingled mostly like their own, with big porches and lawns that needed cutting. Riding became difficult when he turned into a sandy path, deeply furrowed. But it was only a short way to the foot of the dunes, where he dumped his bike and waded uphill through the sand. An immense area of water bordered by a strip of pale sand lay flat and hard before him.

He dropped onto the sand and looked down from the dunes.

"Where is Thatcher Island?" asked Sarah, right behind him.

Naturally she had to follow him.

"Over there." He pointed southeast. "You can't see it from here."

The island was called Thatcher Island after the Thatcher family, who bought it from the Giffords about a hundred years ago. The Giffords had inherited it from the Sears when Nathaniel Sear died and left it to his daughter Mary, who had married a Gifford. Not only Thatcher Island became theirs but a lot of land around Salt Meadow Bay as well. At that time it was known as Gull's Island. The Sears had bartered it from the Indians for a couple of axes and a flintlock gun, which did not last long in the salty air.

Sarah waited for Harry to go on talking, and when he remained silent she wandered toward the water.

Harry knew he shouldn't have come here. Especially since he was only in the intermediate group at swimming lessons and not doing very well. But lying on top of the dunes and staring down at the water always made him forget everything else. Later he would figure out a way to get to Thatcher Island. The white sand under his body, the sounds and smells of the sea reminded him of that afternoon three years ago, and he liked to daydream back, though as he did he shivered a little. He watched Sarah slosh confidently into the waves and then looked for her head bobbing out in the deeper water.

They had all been asleep, tired after a day of driving and eating and playing in the water, with his father teaching him to swim—his mother and father and Sarah and he, Harry, all exhausted and happy. Hadn't he learned the sidestroke today? Done it exactly the way his father wanted him to do it, with breathing every other stroke? Suddenly he had waked up, alarmed. Sarah was gone!

Worried, he had searched for her among the valleys of the dunes and along the beach with its groups of people. When he had found a T-shirt near the water and had seen a head bob up and down past the breaking waves, he had been sure he had spotted her.

"Sarah! Sarah!" he had shouted and, sure of his new skill, he had plunged into the water. It had seemed to him the small figure was waving back and drifting farther away.

Sarah must be riding on a Styrofoam board and she couldn't even swim, only dogpaddle for a couple of feet. Hadn't she been told again and again that it was dangerous to hang on to a surfboard? "Only after you pass the test," his mother had said.

He had to bring her safely back before his parents woke up. He didn't want them upset today. Besides, he knew how to swim, and he was a lot taller. So he walked on the rippled sand deeper into the water. Soon the water reached almost up to his neck and he anticipated each wave with a little jump.

When a particularly strong wave rolled along, it carried him with it and set him adrift. He kicked his legs the way his father had taught him and arched his arms through the water. It surprised him when he sank down after a few short attempts. His feet searched for the bottom and could not find it. Only sinking below the surface did he touch ground. He pushed himself up again in panic, trying to remember what he had learned, but he could not control his arms and legs or make them move in any of the patterns his father had showed him. With all limbs thrashing wildly he broke through the surface. Gulping for breath, he swallowed too much air too soon and lost time and strength coughing and spitting out water before he was able to take another breath and look around for help.

There was nothing but water and the distant beach. "Sarah," he screamed, and the scream seemed to him not louder than a hoarse whisper, utterly useless for summoning help. His arms and legs struggled in vain to keep him afloat and he sank below. Deeper this time,

where the light was feeble and greenish and oddly wel-
coming.

He told himself that he must walk toward the beach,
walk along the bottom of the sea, and he started out in
strange weightless steps that did not touch the ground.
When his chest threatened to burst, he paddled up for
more air. This time he did not bother to call for help
but floated back down and walked on. He surfaced again
and the beach appeared as far away as before. He did not
care. He could not remember why it had been so important to reach it, only that it was important to push
against the sea.

So he went under and flowed with the currents.
When he drifted up once more to breathe, he felt incredibly tired. The water sucked him down; he did not
fight it. Harry was exhausted and sleepy and thought if
he could ease the pain in his chest, all would be well.
Cradled by the water, he was filled with the green light,
dreaming into it, comfortable except for the weight on
his chest, when he remembered Sarah.

"Sarah?" he asked. "Sarah!"

"He's coming around," cried a chorus of voices.

"Sure thought he was a goner."

"The kid is talking! He's alive!"

Harry opened his eyes and the green light of the sea
was gone. Faces stared down at him. One person was
pressing his aching ribs, another pulled his arms up
over his head and yanked them down again to his side.
Now the lifeguard covered his mouth with his own

and blew into him, inflating him with the warm stench of bologna, mustard, lettuce, cheese. A whole submarine sandwich topped off with spearmint gum. Harry tried to fight him off and was immediately subdued. He promised himself never in his life to touch a submarine sandwich.

They said he had needed mouth-to-mouth resuscitation, a word that made his mother cry and his father look pale and serious and Sarah tight-lipped with envy, but Harry was certain that he had needed no such treatment. The lifeguard had probably been showing off to his girl friend. Didn't he blow him up after he had already talked and opened his eyes? A kid as big and heavy as Rhino weighting him down.

Harry trembled as he always did when he remembered the weird green light and then recalled the satisfaction he felt when Sarah was not even scolded for sneaking away and hunting for coins on the parking lot among the cars. In the excitement over him his parents had not noticed she was gone.

"Why did you swim so far out?" Sarah had asked him.

"To save someone's life." He couldn't tell her.

"Then you are a hero."

"Even if there wasn't anybody?"

"Even if there wasn't anybody," Sarah had said firmly. She stood by him.

It was not his fault that he had had to be rescued instead of being able to rescue her. He had not given in without a struggle, had he? A long struggle. Up on top of the dunes he liked feeling like a hero.

And Sarah had been the only one interested in what he had been doing way out there. He should take her along to Thatcher Island. There must be a way. He was going to tell her right now.

But where was she? A moment ago he had seen her swim beyond the waves. Now the water was empty. Harry sat bolt upright, his heart exploding in his ears. He scanned the water, searching the glittering surface. Then he saw her, building a drop castle on the small sandbar to his right where the tidal stream opened into the sea. With an embarrassed laugh he slumped down, turned over, and gazed down into the marsh. Idle, he followed one of the channels with his eyes and soon became wrapped up in tracing the myriad waterways. Ponds and holes and channels and flats were all connected in an intricate pattern with the broad tidal stream that flowed into the ocean a hundred yards away. To amuse himself Harry tried to discover a course he could take from an imagined point in the middle of the marsh to the dunes without getting his feet wet.

"Damn, it must be possible!" he muttered after turning back for the hundredth time to his point of departure. "We did it ourselves, didn't we? With father last fall."

"What are you talking about?" Sarah stood over him, dripping water on his legs. So he explained the game to her.

"But Mr. Walker couldn't do it. Remember, he sank into a deep hole up to his neck. Even his gun got wet." Sarah laughed. Mr. Walker had planned to go duck hunting from the blind near the big flat. "If I take that creek over there . . ." pondered Sarah aloud.

"Quiet," ordered Harry. "You made me lose my track."

They stared at the marsh till Sarah said her eyes were going to pop out of her head if she looked one more minute. "Let's go clamming," she said.

"Your place or mine?"

"Mine's all right."

"You win," said Harry. "If I go to Thatcher Island, you'll come along."

"Oh, Harry," cried Sarah. "We'll check my hole to see if there are enough clams to fill a bucket for the picnic."

<hr>

The Indians had used Thatcher Island as one of their summer campgrounds, the same way they had used other islands. They came to fish and clam, especially during the bluefish season. At spring tides they collected the giant sea clams which are normally covered by six feet of water and more. Huge mounds of shells were left next to their fires.

"Would you send *me* to a friendly town?" asked Sarah the next morning. Again they were sitting together eating breakfast in the kitchen.

"Would you like to go away for a while?" Mrs. Chase spoke from behind her part of the paper.

"It's awfully hot in New York City, ninety-seven degrees and no prospect of cooler weather," announced Mr. Chase from behind his part of the paper.

"Would you send *me* to a friendly town?" repeated Sarah.

"Do you want to visit Aunt Mary in Plymouth for a few days?" Mrs. Chase glanced over the supermarket specials.

"But that's not the same," said Sarah. "I know Aunt Mary."

"I wouldn't call Plymouth a friendly town," put in Mr. Chase. "Remember they gave me a ticket for parking too far away from the curb? One and a half inches, I measured it. First time that ever happened to me! And the long lines at the restaurants! And the prices! Take Sandwich, that's a friendly town."

"You can either visit Aunt Mary in Plymouth or stay with Grandma Carpenter in Boston." Mrs. Chase concentrated on the A&P ads.

"But that's not what I mean," insisted Sarah fiercely. "I *know* them! I've *been* in Boston! I've *been* in Plymouth! Would you send me away as a Fresh Air child?"

"Yes!" said Mrs. Chase, and smiled to show that she

was only teasing. "Yes, I'll send you away this very minute if you don't let me read my paper." In exasperation Sarah looked over to Harry, but he was not listening. Nervously he fingered the keys in his pocket and almost jumped off his chair when they clanked together. Harry was waiting for his father to start his daily hunt for his car keys.

"Harry, if someone was going to pack you off to strangers in New York, what—" began Sarah.

"I think it would be fun," Harry interrupted her quickly. Today he didn't care; he didn't want to think about the Fresh Air kid, he had his own problems, like not letting the right moment slip by. He grimaced at Sarah to shut up.

"Fun?"

"Sure, lots of fun."

He had figured that this was the exact time to approach his father about their plans for Saturday. Later he was going to settle the question about Sarah and the Fresh Air kid with Doug, but his parents came first. His father would be in a hurry to get to work and not as likely to pay much attention to Harry as at another time. Harry felt a little sorry for him, trapped as he was by his son's cleverness. When Mr. Chase put his cup down and folded his paper, he swallowed.

"The Morrisons have asked me and Sarah and the New York kid to come along for a picnic to Thatcher Island on Saturday. Can we go?" Harry was speaking much too fast. Then he realized his mistake. Instead of calling them "Henderson," as he had practiced—Barry Henderson was in his scout troop and safely out of the way traveling with his family—he had let Doug and Patrick's real name slip out along with the name of the island. How stupid of him!

"A picnic, a picnic!" cried Sarah, clapping her hands. "We can go, can't we? Please, dad, mom, let us go!"

Mr. Chase peeled a sticky gumdrop from his fingers and continued his search through the drawers. "We'll talk about it tonight," he said.

This time Harry stayed with his prepared lines. "But I'm supposed to call back this morning."

"Why didn't you let me know last night?" Mr. Chase was cross as he looked over the shelves and felt behind the cookie jar.

"I forgot," said Harry as innocently as he could. He would have to tell Doug the same, which was going to be a lot harder. He pushed the thought away.

"We can go, can't we, dad? You and mom would be free for the day," begged Sarah. "A picnic is so much fun and I do love Thatcher Island and the kid from New York will like it, too. It will be an experience for him, won't it, mom?"

Mrs. Chase had to smile. "If Harry has to call back this morning, we have to give him a definite answer," she remarked. "Your keys are on the piano."

"Not this time." Mr. Chase shook the empty milk bottles and peered into the garbage pail.

"I guess it's all right," he said, defeated. "You telephone the Morrisons, Harry, and tell them how much we appreciate the invitation. Gives mother and me a chance at golf. And tell them we'll speak with them later. Where are those blasted keys?"

Sarah hugged him.

"I'll look for them," cried Harry, rushing out of the kitchen. A moment later he returned with the keys dangling in his hand. His face was flushed.

"Here they are, dad. On the piano just like mother said. But way back under a book." He broke away before his father could thank him.

Sarah talked about Thatcher Island as she cleared the table. "Don't you think it's nice of the Morrisons to invite Harry and me and the Fresh Air kid? They're not even Harry's friends, they're so much bigger. In the tenth grade. Wouldn't you think they would have a spare bed in their huge house? For a Fresh Air kid of their own?"

"What about a spare bed?" inquired Mrs. Chase, skimming the front page. "Why would we need another one?"

"Not us! The Morrisons." Sarah put the bread back into the box. "Thatcher Island is my most favorite island."

Mrs. Chase regarded her absentmindedly. "Is it really," she said.

Harry had waited at his parents' bedroom door till he heard the front door close and Sarah's chatter from the kitchen. Now he walked over to the telephone and dialed.

"This is Harry Wheeler Chase," he said and his throat was dry. "May I speak with Doug or Patrick, please."

"Just a moment." It was Mrs. Morrison on the line. The phone was put down and Harry listened to her distinct voice calling the boys and complaining that she couldn't finish her packing if she had to answer the phone every other minute.

There was a faint comment and the receiver was picked up with a cautious, "Yeah?"

"It's me, Harry," Harry said, jubilant. "I can make it! All went . . ."

"That's great." He was cut short. "We'll phone you back if necessary. Don't call us."

The line went dead. Harry felt deflated. He had wanted them to say "great" as if they really meant it. He had wanted them to be curious about how he had managed to get permission. Apparently they were taking it for granted that anybody, especially Harry, would jump at the chance to be on their team.

It gave Harry a sting that they were right to take him for granted. He was ashamed of his eager voice, his running upstairs to give them the news right away. He should have played it cool, thought about it, and taken the opportunity to hint about his companions, Sarah and the New York kid. Even to ask questions, like how he was supposed to get to the island and what the rules of the game were.

Then it struck him that he had to phone back, though Doug had warned him not to call. It was important. He had to let them know that he had blurted out their name to his parents and that they were likely to speak with Mr. and Mrs. Morrison. His face burned with shame. Reluctantly he lifted the phone and heard his mother talking from the extension in the kitchen. Doug's voice answering shocked him.

"My mother and father aren't here right now," it said, distant and polite. "May I take a message?"

"A picnic on the island is such a marvelous idea," gushed Mrs. Chase. "I wish I could come along." Harry groaned silently, despairing for Doug's answer. There was hardly a pause.

"Why don't you?" He sounded surprisingly friendly. "We are all hoping for an exciting day." Harry admired his smoothness.

"Oh, thank you." That was his mother again. "I think Mr. Chase would prefer some golf. Next time for sure. But you will avoid the channel, won't you? Let your parents know how pleased we are, and if there is anything we can do . . ."

"We'll let you know," continued Doug. "Good-bye, Mrs. Chase. Tell Harry I'll talk with him later."

Harry sighed. At least she had not mentioned Sarah and the Fresh Air kid. Nor had Doug said anything about staying overnight. Perhaps it was just as well that

(26)

Doug had learned from his mother that she knew about Thatcher Island. It took the brunt of responsibility away from him, though he would be careful not to let Doug talk with him too soon.

The Thatcher family did not visit the island often. They took their clams right out of Salt Meadow Bay—sweet bay clams, quahogs, and steamers—and scallops, too. They fished farther south near a group of islands that provided calmer water. They did not like the tricky waters of the channel between the mainland and Baker's Point, where two of the Gifford children, Josh and his cousin Matthew, had disappeared.

Later that day Harry wished for the first time he had never been asked to go to Thatcher Island. He and Sarah had ridden to Quamhassett public beach for their swimming lessons. It would not do to skip twice in a row, though he hated this particular class. They laughed at him. With twenty-five kids in the intermediate group —all of them younger and smaller—he did stick out. But he needed the instruction. It took him so much longer than other kids to learn how to swim. And there were those odd moments he never talked about when his limbs felt heavy and sluggish and pulled him down.

To make matters worse, it was the day of the tryouts for the swimming meet. Twice each summer the best swimmers of each group were selected to compete against winners of other groups on all the different town beaches. Harry didn't care when he came in last and he didn't care very much when the instructor lined them up according to rank and there he was way at the end, like a huge taillight in his red trunks. Then he was called out front.

"Chase, winner of the moon snail award," announced the instructor, presenting him with a live moon snail. Harry stood with clenched teeth while the kids screamed with laughter, the slimy snail on his open palm. More spectators collected. Didn't he see Wesley grinning, Rhino and Gordon towering above a circle of girls?

"You're so mean! So mean!" It was Sarah darting forward and now pummeling their teacher with her fists. The kids doubled their laughter. Harry dropped the snail and dragged her away.

"I hate him, I hate him," she repeated on their way home. "It was such a mean thing to do. Why didn't you do anything?"

"There wasn't anything I could do." Harry shrugged his shoulders. He was not going to attend another class at the public beach. Nobody could force him. He didn't care if he never learned to swim as well as other kids his age. Or as well as Sarah. "Except getting you out of the way before you got hurt. Pretty silly of you." But he winked at her and speeded ahead.

(28)

As Mrs. Chase joined them in the kitchen for lunch, Sarah boasted happily that she had come in fifth at the tryout. "I'll be in advanced intermediate next term," she said. "You should have watched me race. Against Steven and he is good!"

Harry tiptoed out of the kitchen before he could be questioned and fled on his bike. He had to avoid his mother's probing and Sarah's wretched face. He cycled around the harbor, past the grocery store and the fire station, hoping to meet someone he liked—Mike, for example, who was more or less his friend. Or Orrin. Some kids were sailing in the harbor, but he could not make out who they were. Only Frankie was sitting on the bread box in front of the grocery store. Poor dumb Frankie.

"New pants," he said, pointing to his shorts. Harry stopped the bike. "New sneakers." Frankie lifted his dirty tennis shoes, his face happy.

"Nice sneakers," said Harry. "Do you know where Mike is? Mike!"

"Don't know," cried Frankie sadly. Harry noticed that he had quite a lot of hair on his upper lip. Soon he would need a shave. It was funny to think of Frankie grown up and shaving.

"New pants!" Frankie lighted up again as Harry pedaled off.

"Nice pants!"

"Frogs, frogs," shouted Frankie after him, leaping off the bread box and swimming along the sidewalk before climbing back on his seat. He meant Mike was catching frogs at the Black Bog.

Harry skirted the fire station and traveled north. The cranberry bog was about two miles away, at the end of a small road off the main highway, surrounded by woods. Up from the low ridge it looked like a sunken meadow, somewhat reddish with its short-cropped crowded plants, circled by water.

Harry saw nobody near the shed or the ditches but discovered a pair of bikes in the grass where a narrow path led to the abandoned house at the top of Water-man's Creek. So he hid his bike in the underbrush and followed the trail. He was going to surprise them practicing for Thatcher Island.

The first hundred yards he strode ahead, but close to the house he crept forward, gliding from tree to tree with hardly a sound. When he heard Mike and recognized the second voice as Bruce Delaney's, he was glad that nothing had given away his presence. What was Mike doing with Bruce? They weren't friends, were they?

"Got it?"

"Hold it a little higher!"

"Gosh, I'm sinking. We need something larger."

Crouched behind a dead tree, Harry overlooked the muddy pond, the house, and part of Waterman's Creek. Mike and Bruce were building a float, and for the needed pieces of lumber they were hacking away at what had been the living room floor of the abandoned house. Not

(30)

much more was left but the fieldstone foundation, the chimney, and a pile of rotten collapsed boards and planks, partly blackened by fire.

Bruce sent Mike down a hole to pry at the board from underneath while he rested above. He had certainly learned how to boss kids from hanging around with the tenth graders. "Some more muscle, Mike! Give it another push!"

They hauled the board to the water, again with Bruce giving all the orders. Well, Mike must like that! Now he was told where to nail another plank and how to tie two slabs together with string. He, Harry, wouldn't stand for it. Not with Bruce giving the orders. Or Wesley.

"I'll be first," cried Bruce and stepped on the platform. It tilted. Harry pressed a hand against his mouth to stifle his laughter as Bruce stumbled and sank up to his waist in the muddy water. There was not a sound out of Mike. Unseen, Harry returned to the bog.

For a while he hunted frogs. It was fun to scare them into long jumps and sudden dives. When he heard the car, he himself dived into the nearest bush. The cranberry bog was not exactly forbidden territory, but kids were not welcome there.

A pickup truck pushed over the ridge and braked at the shed. Two men got off and entered the building. Excited about another chance to scout, Harry sprinted across the bog, plopped twice into the plants and ended, breathing hard, pressed against the wooden wall of the shed. There was talking inside. He edged near the window, broken long ago and covered with plastic, raised himself and peered through a hole. He saw old Mr. McMurty from the Road Department. The second man he did not know.

Harry dropped on his knees.

"Kids breaking in all the time," said Mr. McMurty.

"What for?"

"That's what I'd like to know. Just fooling around, I guess."

"Nothing to steal, is there?"

"Nothing at all. Wasn't anybody here this time, though."

"How do you know?"

There was a clatter of metal. Harry hoisted himself back to his peephole.

"The cans! I arranged them in special order right behind the door and they're just the way I left them, so there wasn't anybody here."

They cackled, delighted. Now Mr. McMurty bent over a tool chest. Suddenly his body jerked, he jumped up and down, howling, and danced in small steps with the left hand supporting his right arm. Harry saw something oblong and dark swinging from his right hand. A trap, big and powerful enough to catch the largest rat for good, was clamped firmly around the old man's fingers. Harry ducked down.

"Hold still a minute! Let me get it off."

"Ouch," bawled Mr. McMurty. But apparently he

stood still long enough to have the trap removed.

"It's a strong one. Could have broken your fingers."

"Might be nipped, one or two of them bones," he groaned. "Damn kids."

"You figure who did it?"

"Have a pretty good idea. Chased off the Morrison boys the other day. Damn nuisance, those boys."

Harry pulled himself up for a last look, one foot on a shaky board.

"Remember the shed on Cremer's Bog that went up in flames one night?"

"Yeah, was around this time of the year."

"Were local kids all right. Who else would wander around Cremer's Bog in the middle of the night?" Now old Mr. McMurty lowered his voice and Harry leaned forward. "Me and Patrolman Schwendiman had a beer together. A lot of kids weren't home that night. Some game, he said. His own wasn't home either. Spent the night with the Morrisons. Came back with one eye swollen shut."

"Didn't use the third degree, did he?" Both men chuckled.

Harry lost his balance and bumped into the wooden wall. The noise was enormous, hollow and full. He sprang up, zigzagging over the bog.

"Stop, boy, stop!" they shouted after him. Harry thought of Gordon Schwendiman and his lazy voice. *Hunt him?*

And here he was being chased across the bog. He ran

faster. As he skidded and fell he wished for a moment he had never been asked to be part of the team on Thatcher Island. Then he dashed on.

In the safety of the woods he waited till the old men drove off. The trap hidden in the chest had been a neat trick. What fun to watch it happen. What a dance McMurty had done. Served him right for gossiping about Doug and Patrick. Old McMurty had no proof they had started the fire on purpose. He was only guessing. He didn't even know for sure they were out that night. Nothing but rumors, though a lot of damage had been done.

As he went for his bike Harry was suddenly glad he wasn't allowed to stay out overnight. Not with Sarah and the kid from the city. Not on Thatcher Island with Doug Morrison and his team.

Thatcher Island had been left to itself till Robert Thatcher came along and explored the Indian campsites some eighty years ago. Sites one and two lay protected in the coves where the more prominent head of the island narrowed into its long body. Site three was situated near Baker's Point at the tip of the island. It was here that Robert Thatcher liked to camp, lighting his fire near the mound

*of shells, watching the lights of Salt Meadow Farm
in the evening.*

Wednesday the Morrisons picked him up soon after
lunch. In the morning Harry had helped to get his room
ready—cleared the table, emptied one drawer of his
chest of drawers. Fresh linen for the bed. The blue
blanket out of the hall closet.

"Shouldn't Harry hide his stamp collection?" Sarah
asked.

"Why, Sarah?" asked her mother gently. "Why
do you say that, Sarah?"

And Sarah stumbled right on. "So he wouldn't steal
them!"

They were in for another of her long reasonable talks
while Harry studied his favorite model, a destroyer he
had glued together last Christmas. One of the anti-air-
craft guns needed regluing. Then he saw his father's
Swiss army knife on the shelf. He had borrowed it
secretly some days ago and he hoped she wouldn't discover it. Meanwhile Sarah scratched between her toes.

"Now, Sarah, will you please get the towels?" finished Mrs. Chase.

"I wouldn't leave the valuable ones around if I were
you, Harry," hissed Sarah in a loud whisper as she
passed him on her errand. But his mother had run out
of words. She did not call her back.

They had just cleared the table after lunch when

(35)

there was a perfunctory knock at the front door and Doug and Patrick Morrison walked in.

"I hope we aren't disturbing you, Mrs. Chase, but we would like a little chat with Harry." As always it was Doug who did the talking.

"So many preparations," exclaimed Mrs. Chase. "You'll have a wonderful time. It's so nice of you and your parents to ask Harry and . . ."

"Can I go?" Harry was already halfway through the door. "I'll be home later!" He couldn't let his mother and Doug keep on talking.

"Good-bye, Mrs. Chase."

"Bring him back in time for supper, Doug!"

Harry walked between Doug and Patrick down the drive. It seemed like a long walk and not a word was spoken. Gordon Schwendiman and Rhino were waiting in the VW bus on the road, grinning at him.

"Chase, didn't we tell you to keep quiet?" Gordon said. "And what does your old lady do but call up the Morrisons to get herself invited. Doug said he considered taking her along, but she had another date. Wasn't that too bad!" They all laughed.

Harry stood silent, his head bowed. He was sure they were going to kick him out of the game.

"I don't like it," grumbled Rhino. "Some big mouth."

"It's all right, Chase." Doug slapped his shoulders hard. "It's quite all right. Doesn't make a bit of difference. They always know where we are, though usually after the fact."

(36)

More laughter. Grateful, Harry looked up at Doug.

"Come on, get in!" He was pushed up into the front seat, where he sat between the Morrison boys. "You'll help us get ready."

Harry sat with his head high and his shoulders straight so that people in other cars and on the sidewalk could see him among his companions. He was one of the team, his blunder forgiven.

They cruised along Main Street, circled the high school, and drove back the same route. When Harry saw Bruce crossing the street, he lifted his chin. Doug pulled up next to him.

"Get us some ice cream, Bruce." He leaned out of the window. "Four cones with two scoops each. Vanilla-butterscotch, chocolate chip-coffee, toasted almond-blueberry. What's your favorite, Chase?"

Harry almost stammered. "Raspberry sherbet and French vanilla."

"You got it, Bruce? French vanilla."

Bruce Delaney nodded and flew off.

The ice cream tasted better than ever. Harry licked his slowly to make it last, while Bruce watched them eat. He did not eat himself, he only watched. Neither did Rhino. He was on another diet, he explained, a muscle-building diet. He flexed his arm.

"Now let's go to work." Doug dropped his half-eaten cone into the gutter.

"You know, Chase," Rhino said, putting his mouth close to Harry's ear, "Doug found a spider at the bottom of his cone. Not long ago. A black hairy thing. Huge, too. It was simply gross." He shook himself, sickened.

Harry licked on. He did not believe Rhino's story. Anyway, packed between Doug and Patrick, he did not dare to get rid of his cone. He could hear Rhino burst into laughter. But the ice cream tasted flat.

Doug started the bus and drove through the town to the parking lot of the big shopping center. "Here?" he asked.

The lot was empty under the midday sun; only near the drugstore a number of cars were clustered.

"Seems all right," said Gordon. "Why don't you park with the rest of them, with your nose to the exit."

They climbed out of the bus.

"We need rope, adhesive tape, safety pins, matches, batteries, several flashlights. We'll take three or four, I think." Doug consulted a list. "The rest of the stuff later at the market with the food and drink."

"Chase, you get matches and two rolls of tape," directed Gordon.

"Money," said Harry meekly. "I don't have any money with me."

Only Gordon heard him. The others walked ahead.

"Don't you worry about money!" He was smirking. Then he joined the group in front. Harry thought of running away. They wouldn't hold him, would they?

He had been told to steal and he couldn't do it. He stood, chewing his lip. As his friends entered the five-and-ten, Doug turned and waved. Harry raced after them. Here was his chance to make up for his mistake. Besides, matches and tape were nothing valuable.

They had spread over the store, examining different counters. Harry watched Doug pick up a roll of string, drawing it apart to test its strength. The manager approached him and Doug conferred with him. That must have been the signal because now Gordon and Patrick and Rhino stopped drifting and aimed for specific counters.

He had to move too. Harry longed to crawl through the aisle, but wasn't that even more suspicious? He went forward on wobbly legs. If he was caught? What about the police? His parents? SHOPLIFTERS WILL BE PROSE-CUTED said a sign. Nevertheless he reached the counter with the drugs. The tape was up on a special board. A tiny cylinder of tape fastened to a giant piece of cardboard under a cover of plastic. And he wore nothing but his jeans and T-shirt with no place to hide anything larger than a matchbox. He looked around for help, saw Doug still engaged with the manager and Patrick smiling at two salesgirls. Forgetting the hidden cameras, Harry lunged up, tore the cardboard down, and tried to rip the plastic off.

It squeaked.

Startled, he stuffed the incriminating piece under his shirt. Everybody must have observed him. He waited for a hand on his shoulder. When nothing happened, he rearranged the cardboard under his armpit and boldly rushed up to the checkout counter.

(39)

"I couldn't find the type of paper I wanted," said Harry, twisted sideways, his voice low.

"What were you looking for?" The girl at the counter was doing her nails, filing at her pinkie.

"A notebook with blue and red and yellow pages." Now Doug and the others had lined up behind him.

"We don't carry that." The girl beamed at Doug. "Hi, Doug!"

Harry was shoved aside. Gordon and Patrick and Rhino dumped rolls of tape, the rope, the matches, the safety pins, the batteries and the flashlights on the counter and the girl rang each item on the register. Doug presented her with the money. She handed him the brown paper bag with the purchase. He passed the bag to Gordon, who passed it to Harry. As Harry reached for it, the stolen tape slipped out from under his shirt and landed on the floor in front of the counter for all to see. Only the cashier was busy beaming at Doug.

Immediately Gordon Schwendiman kneeled on top of the tape, fixing his shoelaces. He scooped it up and let it disappear behind his broad back. "What did you do that for?" he asked softly, nudging Harry through the door. He was grinning.

Harry did not know what to say. Admit another mistake? Doug had never meant him to lift the tape. Or the matches. And he wasn't even sure if Gordon had set him up.

"You got some nerve, Chase." It was Doug at his side.

(40)

"We should have let him get all the stuff!" Rhino punched Harry's chest. "Would have been a lot cheaper."

Harry basked in their company all afternoon. Sarah was waiting for him, concealed by the fence, when they let him out of the bus.

"I wouldn't like to meet them in the dark." Sarah squinted after the bus. "Maybe—"

Harry cut her off. "So you changed your mind? You aren't coming to Thatcher Island?"

"I guess Doug Morrison is all right," said Sarah. "He sure can talk mom into anything. But I don't like the others."

Harry did not defend them. He looked down the road where the bus had vanished and saw them: big, powerful, at times ugly and menacing and perhaps dangerous. Nonetheless for him they ranked first. They carried weight, their team counted, and he had to be part of it. He brushed away the moments of acute embarrassment. It had always been his fault, hadn't it? Some stupid mistake.

"You'll have nothing to do with them," he said. "You promised you'd stay with the Fresh Air kid."

They went inside.

PART
2

Thatcher Island was said to be haunted. Years ago people had talked about a column of smoke that warned fishermen about impending storms; some believed they had seen an Indian girl stoke a fire. Others had reported sighting a sailor in outlandish clothing out on the beach of the eastern cove in the last light before rain and wind swept down on them. So the eastern cove was known as Signal Cove and the western one named after the Giffords.

John caught a glimpse of the island as the bus swerved off the highway into the winding road that led to Egham and the bus depot. It was a dark line on top of the silvery water. A faint column of smoke trailed above it, rising from a steamer on its way south. He did not think about it. He was not interested in the countryside; he was watching for people, houses, cars, signs of human activities. John needed to know as much as he could about the town before he got off the bus and met his hosts. The skin on his face felt tight.

"You are going to camp," his mother had said, and he had been ashamed for her that she had lied to him and angry with himself for pretending to believe her. He knew he was not going to camp. Camp was something you paid for or won a scholarship to, and you lived in the mountains in tents, just kids together with a couple of counselors.

John was not going to camp. He had been selected by the Fresh Air Fund to stay with strange people at their house, eat at their table, sleep in one of their beds. He should have told his mother that he did not want to go, that she should send Randy or Walter, his brothers, or his sister Clarissa, but he could not hurt her. She had been happy for him and he could not tell her that he hated what she had done: She had begged for charity. Signed off and tagged, they had traveled since early in the morning, a whole busload of kids between six and twelve years old. His tag read "Egham" and "Chase" and his own name, "John Forrester." Soon after departing from the city with a stupendous uproar, everyone had fallen into a sort of daze, chewing, sleeping, humming, mooning, but at the first stop they had sat alert. The man in charge had thumbed through a list, called a number of names, and told the kids to pack up.

"It's your stop," he had said cheerfully. "Isn't it a beautiful place? You'll like it."

He had had to repeat the names three times before their owners had struggled up from their seats, flustered and unhappy. John had watched them stumble along the aisle with their sweaters and lunch bags and comics and emerge, their faces vacant. They had been surrounded, their tags had been fingered, and then they had been steered to separate little groups.

As the bus drove on, the rest of them had started to shout.

"Hey, man, did you see that old buggy? Falling to pieces!"

"And that mean-looking bag with the pink curlers! Boy, am I glad I didn't get her!"

"Yours will be worse. Just you wait!"

"See them kids staring at us? Hicks!"

"I hate spinach and green beans! I hate it, I hate it!" the little kid next to John had cried and then had laughed when John had told him: "Why don't you puke it all over them!"

"Gee, it doesn't look so great around here! Let's go back!"

"Yeah, yeah! Let's go back!" they had howled together.

The bus had not turned around. The man in charge had treated their demand as a joke, laughing till they had grown silent.

Ever since they had passed the sign TOWN OF EGHAM John had studied the scene outside intently. Nothing impressed him. The houses were sparse and not imposing, the yards littered with boats and lumber, bikes, toys, and rusty swingsets, the kids dressed as he was, the roads full of pickup trucks, station wagons, and battered small buses.

He hated the people waiting for him. They were part of a whole world that was out to humiliate him. Like the agency his mother had applied to and the men and women with their lists and tags and stupid smiles. Like the man on the bus who passed himself off as their friend. Giving something for free! There is nothing free, as everybody knows. You have to pay by being grateful if you have nothing else to pay with. John was determined not to be grateful for anything.

They rode through a stretch of woods, passed into a busy street, and before there was time to examine the low shops, the bus veered into the yard of the depot. People stood waiting in tight chatty circles. John walked straight through the aisle and stepped down. He fixed his eyes firmly on the space ahead. Someone reached for his tag.

"Mrs. Chase, your boy!"

He was prodded toward a vague form. Before the face took shape, he lowered his eyes and examined the tartan pants, the white sandals, the pink toenails. He hated pink toenails. Then he looked up, ready to stare her down.

(48)

"Hi, John."

Wide perfect teeth greeted him and a hand with pink nails steered him over to where Harry and Sarah stood, scraping the ground.

"This is John," Mrs. Chase informed them gaily. "I am sure we will all have a very good time together."

Harry and Sarah studiously avoided looking at John. They had watched the bus arrive and had followed with their eyes every kid coming down the steps and into the gathering of grown-ups.

"That girl looks nice," Sarah had said. "Why can't I have a spare bed in my room?"

"You think she wouldn't touch your doll's house?" Harry had teased her.

"I might have changed my mind," Sarah had replied haughtily. "See that skinny kid over there! Doesn't he look scared!"

"So would you."

"Not when I'm as big as he is. He has nothing but a shopping bag. Watch out, it's going to bust." Sarah had begun to giggle.

"That's because he's poor."

"I know that too, stupid. Still, it would be funny!"

"That's ours! The one with the striped T-shirt." Harry had inspected the blank face with the sternly shut mouth. The boy had been wooden, letting the adults handle him any way they wanted. Was he going to be trouble on the island?

"He's shorter than you are, Harry. Do you think

we'll like him?" Sarah had sounded suddenly anxious.

"It's only for two weeks," he had told her.

As Mrs. Chase got behind the wheel, she did not seem to take notice of the three doubtful faces, each trying to appear indifferent. Harry and Sarah glanced out of the window. John was fingering the card around his neck with his name on it.

"The bus was late. We had to wait more than an hour," said Mrs. Chase and started the car. "You will like it here, John." John decided she was blaming him for making her wait so long. He moved to the edge of the seat, nursing his hatred. With his forehead pressed against the glass of the window he saw nothing but intense green brushed golden by the sunlight rushing past.

"I bet the traffic was heavy," said Harry. "Boy, it must have been hot, sitting in the bus all day."

"It was pretty hot waiting here," added Sarah.

There was no comment from John.

Harry glanced over to the Fresh Air kid and saw him close to the window. He had a crescent scar on the back of his head, whitish, about an inch and a half long, visible through the long brown straight hair. A large juice can, Hawaiian Punch or V-8, thought Harry. His shoulders looked peaked under the thin shirt and his shoulder blades were clearly marked. He was narrow and wiry and not much shorter than Harry, though that was hard to judge because of the way he crouched. He appeared sullen. Harry would have liked to say something, but nothing came to his mind. So he, too, peered out the window till they arrived.

"Here we are," cried Mrs. Chase. "Feel right at home, John."

"I'll show you the room," mumbled Harry, and walked ahead with John's suitcase.

John climbed out slowly. Everything around him was distinct with sharp black lines. The large gray house, covered with shingles, the windows on each side of the front door, which was framed with white pillars and a triangular board. The tire on a rope, hanging motionless from the big chestnut tree. Then he followed Harry into the house and up the stairs.

"Yours." Harry gestured toward a bed and chest of drawers. After a long, awkward silence he escaped, leaving John sitting dumbly on the blue blanket.

John counted the days. They added up to thirteen if he skipped the day they were going to leave. Or twelve because the first day had almost run out. Not very long really. He moved his eyes over the room, the shelves with the books and games, the record player on the floor, the other bed with its blue spread matching the wallpaper. He liked the room. For such a short time he could live with anybody as long as they were not trying to put him down.

He walked over to the window. A big tree filled up most of the view, but at the left corner was a stretch of dark green, topped off by a line of silver: the ocean. When John spotted the tree house, hidden in the lower branches, his eyes gleamed.

Robert Thatcher built his cabin between site one and site two right in the middle of the slender neck of the island. He had camped for three summers on Thatcher Island and wanted a more permanent base. It took him months to ferry the logs across and do the construction work. He had planned a two-room cabin. Shortly after he had finished the building, the hurricane of 1879 blew across the island. Robert Thatcher perished in the storm and, since few of his possessions were ever found, talk about a concealed cellar or cache did not die.

When Sarah spied upon John some time later, he stood near the shelf and held Harry's model destroyer in his hand.

"What are you doing with Harry's destroyer?" asked Sarah.

"I wasn't going to break it," said John coldly, and went back to the bed and looked at her. Alone with her, he did not mind inspecting her closely. She was smaller than his sister Clarissa and her hair was lighter but just as long and just as tangled. She had freckles on her cheeks and her nose was peeling.

"I am Sarah Chase," she said, glaring at him. "Why don't you stop your stupid staring?"

"And what are you doing?"

"That's because I've never seen you before," explained Sarah.

"And have I seen you anyplace?"

Sarah laughed. "No."

Then she said very formally with a small bow in his direction: "Excuse me if I was rude."

John scowled at her. "Who told you to say that?"

"My mother."

"Why?"

"Because you're a guest!"

"A guest," snorted John, and retreated to the window. "Is that your tree house?"

Sarah at his side nodded. "It's our old one. It's falling apart. Harry lets me use it. He's building another one way back."

"Why don't you fix it up?"

"I don't know how," said Sarah. "Do you?"

"I guess so," said John, leaning farther out of the window.

"You want to see it?"

"Sure," said John, and ran after her, down the stairs, through the hall, and out the front door.

"Sarah, do you know where Harry is?" Mrs. Chase called as they passed the kitchen.

"No," shouted Sarah without stopping. She was trotting around the house toward the big tree. It formed a tent with its branches sagging almost to the ground. Entering the green curtain, John realized that the tree house was in bad shape. Most of its boards were cracked, split, or rotten.

"Needs some new planks," he said. "Shouldn't be difficult."

"And a seat," requested Sarah.

"A seat, a large seat," repeated John wistfully.

"Let's have a look at Harry's new one!" Sarah directed him deeper into the yard, around patches of shrubs to a group of large trees. Rungs of a primitive ladder were nailed to the trunk of the middle tree. Its lower and upper branches were perfect for supporting a tree house, widespread and sturdy. But not much work had been done yet and the house was far from finished. As John reached for the lowest rung to climb up, he found himself with a piece of wood in his hand. The nail had come off. The next one was loose too and the third splintered. There was no way to get up.

"We'll repair it later," said Sarah. "First I'll show you around."

John hesitated, then he tailed after her. He would have liked to start work on the tree house right away. A real tree house! And he was good with tools. But he did not want to give himself away.

At a shed, small and shingled like the big house, Sarah pointed to a monstrously big black bike. "You can take dad's bike! We'll ride around."

"I'm hungry." John was determined. "I didn't get anything on the bus, so I'm starved." He needed time to practice alone on the big bike.

"Peanut butter or graham crackers?" asked Sarah. John was a guest and guests could not walk all over the kitchen and help themselves.

"Peanut butter."

Sarah ran back.

Now was his opportunity. John seized the handlebars and pushed the bike for a few steps to feel it move. The surface of the drive was smooth and the bike rolled easily.

He stopped and glanced around. Trees and bushes sheltered him from the house. He was alone. Now one foot touched the pedal tentatively, then he stepped on it and pushed off. The wheels spun along the drive and John clung to the handlebars, struggling to get one leg over to the other side, but as much as he twisted his body, he could not do it. He had used the wrong leg. He, himself, had been in the way.

Once more he checked his surroundings. Now he tried again, launched himself off, landed in the seat. Not terribly secure, but with both feet on the right pedals. He gripped the bars and pedaled fiercely.

The wheels turned faster and faster. The bike zigzagged along the driveway. John wobbled too far to the right, wheeled madly to the left, curved around, thought himself saved but had already lost control. A bush loomed large in front of him.

He closed his eyes and scooted straight into it. Leaves brushed his face, branches grabbed for his clothes. Something sharp threatened to pierce his stomach. The bike stood motionless on its own two wheels, propped up from both sides by dense green. John opened his eyes. Just inches away was the startled face of Harry.

"I can explain everything," muttered Harry, flustered. "I really can."

John's clenched fist wavered before Harry's eyes. He withdrew as far as he could, but the bush would not let him slip away. What a great beginning. John wouldn't hit him, or would he? He was a guest!

"I can explain everything," Harry said again and kept his eyes on the fist as it swung back and forth. "I wasn't spying on you. Honest. I was . . ." He faltered. How could he tell the Fresh Air kid that he had been too embarrassed to watch him any longer sitting on the bed with his glum face. That he had searched his mind for anything to say and found nothing but stupid phrases like: "How do you like it here?" and "Did you have a good trip?" or "What grade are you in?"

So he had gone into hiding and was caught in this ridiculous situation. But John's heading straight for the bush had been funny, too. The way he hung on to the bike, swatting the air with the wrong leg. Everybody had trouble with his father's bike the first time around. It was too big.

Harry began to laugh. Sort of hysterically at first

and then without constraint. Furiously John swiped his right at him, but he had already flung himself down and was buried somewhere in the bush. John could hear his choked laughter.

He got stiffly off the bike and pushed out of the thicket, ignoring Harry, who crawled after him. He would not hit anybody who was on the ground. Besides, Harry had looked scared. So he jumped into the saddle and pedaled along the driveway in a beautiful straight line, disappearing from sight around the bend.

"But I just happened to be here," Harry cried after him. "And I wasn't laughing at you. I wasn't really!"

"Then what were you laughing about?" asked Sarah. She carried a peanut butter and jelly sandwich. "Where's John?"

John came cycling back, rode up to them, stopped abruptly, and tilted sideways in slow motion. For a moment he had forgotten that you cannot keep your balance without moving. Glued to the seat, his hands firmly on the bars, he and the bike plummeted to the ground together.

"What a fall!" said Sarah admiringly. "I wish I could do that!"

She let herself fall forward but just before striking the pavement her arms shot out to brake the impact.

"It's not as easy as it looks," said John, getting up. "It needs a lot of willpower."

Harry burst into another round of laughter, pointing at the sticky white and brown and purple lump in

Sarah's hand, and John and Sarah had to laugh too as she wiped the gooey stuff off in the grass.

"And I put lots and lots of grape jelly on it, our own." Sarah licked her fingers.

"I'll get another one," offered Harry.

"Never mind now," said John. He wasn't hungry. He hadn't been hungry earlier. He had needed time to learn how to ride a bike alone. "Let's ride around till supper." He glared at Harry to challenge him.

"Race you to the big elm and back," Harry proposed earnestly.

"Mine has a flat," declared Sarah. "Anyway I was going to show John the dinghy I found last year."

Robert Thatcher had used a dinghy to carry him from the mainland to the island and back. The same winds that blew his cabin apart took the boat and hurled it across the water into Salt Meadow Bay, depositing it with a lot of other debris almost at the front door of Salt Meadow Farm. For quite some time they waited for him to come back and claim his boat. When he never did, they filled it with tubs of geraniums, though they could easily have dragged it back into the bay. It had been and still was a good boat.

(58)

"So you are John, our guest from the big city," said Mr. Chase, and patted his shoulder. Sarah and Harry stood close to their father, watching John.

"I hope you brought a large appetite. Or don't you like fried chicken?"

John nodded. Normally he could not get enough of fried chicken but it was difficult to like it today with everybody looking at him. And questioning him. Harry and Sarah too regarded him curiously, as if they had not laughed together before. Every mouthful stuck to his palate and teeth while he examined their questions.

Yes, he had two brothers and one sister. Their names were Randy, Walter, and Clarissa.

Sarah giggled; she had never heard the name Clarissa and to her it sounded like something to freshen the throat.

No, he did not know what Randy stood for. Just Randy.

Yes, he was the oldest.

No, he had never been away from New York.

"I've been in Europe," said Sarah. "I've been in eight different countries. England . . ."

"Oh, shut up, Sarah," grumbled Harry, though he would rather have listened to her than to John's grudging answers. He was being put on the spot.

"What does your father do? Where does he work?" asked Mrs. Chase. "Mr. Chase is with the local oil company."

"We sell oil to the whole town, for heating homes

and schools and offices," Mr. Chase stated. "We service furnaces and even clean chimneys."

"Belgium, Holland, France . . ." singsonged Sarah.

"Be quiet, Sarah!" Mrs. Chase's voice was sharp. "John was telling us about his father. Go on, John."

John looked up from his plate straight into Mrs. Chase's eyes. Harry noticed it, because John had been picking at his food before.

"He works at a garage. Cardozo's. He's a mechanic," said John, staring at Mrs. Chase. "He is over six feet tall, he played basketball real good in high school, he made the school team each year. He takes me and Randy and Walter and Clarissa to the zoo on Sundays. Or the park. He teaches me and Randy how to throw a curve ball. He shows us how to fix things up like broken furniture and building a cart for Walter. And my mother works at Central. She's a nurse."

John clenched his jaws together and bent over his plate. Harry knew that something was wrong—John had spoken much too fast and much too fluently, as if he had rehearsed the part. He had probably lied. Only why should he have lied about his parents?

"They must make a lot of money together. Then I don't understand . . ." speculated Sarah, but her father cut her off.

"It's been hot in New York this summer," he said. "Hotter than usual."

John nodded, while Sarah continued cheerfully. "Switzerland, Italy, Denmark."

(60)

"That's only seven," John said, and Harry observed how sharp he was, counting along with Sarah while watching the rest of the family.

"Austria," said Mrs. Chase as if it were really important. "You couldn't forget that lovely old farmhouse in the mountains, all painted and carved, could you, Sarah?" She was clearly irritated, glancing over to Mr. Chase, who shook his head. Harry knew she was irritated because of the money. John was obviously just as well off as they were, and that left her hanging with all her words about helping and sharing with the poor.

"Austria," repeated Sarah, and John smiled at her. He was content to have scored his point. He had made it clear to all members of the Chase family that he by no means needed their charity. He did not care if they felt cheated now.

"John should finish your tree house, Harry," said Sarah. "He says he can do it, didn't you, John?"

John bowed his head; he was not going to show them he was interested in any of their affairs. Still, he did not like Harry's careless answer.

"After Thatcher Island," he said.

"Thatcher Island, that reminds me! I met Charles Morrison at lunch today at the Parson's Elm." Mr. Chase turned to Harry, who was choking on his potato.

Harry coughed and gripped the seat of his chair with a sickening feeling in the pit of his stomach. Now it was his turn to be scrutinized, and he was not going to stand up as well as John to probing questions. Questions like how come Harry hadn't told them it was just a children's party? And why did Mr. and Mrs. Morrison know nothing about it? In fact, they were going away over the weekend.

"Isn't it funny we both never mentioned the picnic on Thatcher Island? I thought I heard him say that he was leaving on business, but he must have meant the week after." Mr. Chase chuckled, and Harry gave a shrill cry of relief.

They played Clue after supper. Mr. and Mrs. Chase withdrew with their papers in front of the TV and came back from time to time to nod approvingly over the game. It took Harry a while to realize that John had engaged in the same strategy as he himself: letting Sarah win without allowing her to suspect an easy victory.

"You're cheating," Sarah accused them both when she caught them moving a piece to her advantage. "I'm not playing any more."

"Oh, come on, Sarah," cried Harry. "We promise, we'll stay clean."

So they played according to the rules and Sarah won handily.

Later, in bed, Harry asked John if he had ever been to an island and was disappointed when John said, "Sure."

"Where?"

"Manhattan. That's where I live."

"I mean a real island with water all around," explained Harry.

"Like the one with the Statue of Liberty?" John wanted to know. "We made a trip over there with a boat. You do need a boat. Doreen got sick and puked over two seats and old bag Flanigan was out of her mind because she couldn't get the numbers right. There she was counting and counting and there were always two kids less on the way back. Boy, was she worried sick! She didn't even mind Doreen."

It sounded like a normal class trip, but since he was obviously expected to ask after the two kids, Harry did.

"Did they fall overboard or something?"

"Fats Dominguez had locked two tourists under his armpits on the way over so they got counted by mistake."

Harry laughed briefly.

"I mean another sort of island, more like Robinson Crusoe's."

"Robinson who?"

"Robinson Crusoe. You must know him! He was shipwrecked and lived alone on an island. He's famous."

"Oh, the guy on TV." John dismissed him and the whole show. "Why should I want to go to an island like that? With no people? What would I be doing there all by myself?"

Nevertheless he paid attention to Harry's fervent voice as he went on talking about Thatcher Island and the bluefish and the Indians and the clams and the hurricane and Robert Thatcher and his cabin and the fact

that some people were still searching for his lost be-
longings.

"What kind of people?" asked John.

"People like Sarah."

They both did not mention the treasure again.

"We'll have a picnic on the island," said Harry.

"With Robinson?" joked John, but when Harry said
their names were Morrison, Doug and Patrick Morrison, and they had nothing to do with Robinson
Crusoe, as if John couldn't distinguish between what
was real and what was on TV, he pulled the blanket
over his head and let Harry rattle on into the silent
room.

"We'll bring something to eat and drink, build a
fire, roast hamburgers and hot dogs and perhaps clams,
drink Coke or Sprite or whatever you like. Though
there is a small sweet-water swamp on the island. You
can drink the water. It's perfectly safe." Then Harry
remembered that the picnic had been totally Sarah's idea
and he was quiet.

*Robert Thatcher had counted on the water in the
swamp to supply him with drinking water. He had
begun to enlarge the basin and line it with rocks
at the bottom and the sides. The basin had formed
at the lowest point of the swamp. He had cleared*

(64)

the plants away, cattails and water lilies and reed
grass. After his disappearance the plants moved
back, pushing their roots between the rocks, break-
ing the open surface of the water. Only a particu-
larly large boulder kept a small area open. It was
here that the birds came to drink and bathe.

There were piles of pancakes for breakfast and John
and Harry and Sarah covered them with butter and
poured syrup over their stacks and ate. The sun played
with the leaves and branches of the apple tree and threw
changing patterns of light on the table.

"Don't forget your swimming lessons," Mrs. Chase
reminded them.

"There aren't any lessons today because of the meet,"
said Harry. "But we can swim at the dunes, can't we?"

Mrs. Chase nodded, smiling.

"Ride your bikes and take good care of John. Don't
let him swim out too far. You can swim, can't you,
John?"

"Yes," said John. They were not going to find out
that he couldn't, not this morning, nor that he didn't
have swimming trunks. Upstairs in the bathroom he
fashioned a pair out of his jeans by amputating the legs
with a knife he had seen on Harry's shelf. It was hard
work cutting through the tough fabric and left him
with only his brown Sunday slacks and the pants he
wore. The trunks' legs were uneven, one reaching almost to his knee. He pulled it up, pasted a couple of

Band-Aids on his thigh and pulled the cloth down.

They cycled past the meadows and woods to the marsh.

"Cattails," said Sarah, pointing to the extremely tall grass next to the road. "You can eat them."

"Taste like asparagus," added Harry.

"Better!"

"That's our marsh." Harry waved his arm over the whole area of dark green moist meadow. "That's where we get cherrystones and other stuff. We'll dig some later."

"It stinks," remarked John. "Why does it stink?"

"It doesn't stink," protested Sarah. "It smells like marsh. I like it." She led into the sandy path. They dumped their bikes at the foot of the dunes and ran up, with the sand giving way under their feet.

"That's our beach! Now let's go into the water."

"Last one in does the dishes," cried Sarah, and she and Harry stormed downhill. John dropped into the sand at the top of the dunes. They called to him but he did not stir. So finally Sarah came back.

"I'll help you with the dishes," she promised, shaking her wet tangled hair like a dog.

John exposed the row of Band-Aids. To him they looked suspiciously clean and new. "I shouldn't go in the water."

"What is it?" She bent over him, dripping.

"It's a cut," explained John.

(66)

"A cut? What a big one! It must have bled an awful lot!" Sarah shuddered. "How did you get it? Did you fall on something sharp?"

"Someone knifed me." It was the first thing that came to his mind. Sarah stood with her mouth open.

"Kni—knifed you!" she breathed. "Tell me all about it! Was it a real fight like on TV?"

"Just a fight." John tried to tone it down.

"I thought," said Sarah slowly. "I mean, mother said they send only good kids out of the city. She said they screen you carefully to see if you need and deserve it. They wouldn't send kids who got into trouble."

"They made a mistake." John's answer was cold and sharp. He rolled on his stomach and stared into the marsh. His mouth tasted bitter, though he had won another point. He had been right to hate charity, since there were so many reservations attached to it: You had to be poor, you had to be grateful, you had to be good. He badly wished that it had been a genuine wound, received in a genuine fight.

Meanwhile Harry had returned and Sarah was telling him about it.

"A real fight like on TV," she said. "With knives. And John got a cut that big!" She measured three, four inches with her fingers.

"How many stitches?" Harry wanted to know. What if the wound opened and started to bleed? What if that happened Saturday on the island?

"They shouldn't have sent him," Sarah went on. "But I don't mind. Just think, they could have sent somebody like Fraser."

John glared at her angrily. "Who's Fraser?"

"Some kid in school who doesn't wash. Never! He smells something terrible. If you think our marsh stinks, you should take a whiff of him sometime. I'll try to arrange that." Sarah laughed.

"Then I'm glad I'm not Fraser." John grinned up at her.

"Why should we mind?" cried Harry, excited. He was sure a knife wound did not occur out of the blue. John was a real tough kid from the city. It meant a change in his plans. Now he was going to present John to Doug and Patrick, Rhino, Gordon and the others as an asset to the team, a fighter. How much easier it was going to be to meet them at the dock! "The wound, it's almost healed, isn't it?"

Harry was assured that the cut needed no special care except to be kept dry. "Why should we mind?" he cried again. "But mother and dad wouldn't like it. They'll fuss over it, so let's keep it a secret."

"They might not let you go to Thatcher Island," said Sarah. "If they knew."

Sarah had a weakness for secrets and rarely betrayed them.

John nodded solemnly. He couldn't afford to have anybody look under the Band-Aids. Neither Mr. and Mrs. Chase nor Harry and Sarah. But he wondered about Harry. Wasn't he sort of overreacting to a simple thing like a cut?

Back at the house, they passed through a difficult moment at lunch. Mrs. Chase had prepared sandwiches and chips and fruit and filled tall glasses with milk.

"Dad can't find his Swiss army knife," she said. "You know, the one with the red handle. You didn't borrow it by chance and forget to give it back? You know he doesn't like that."

The word "knife" launched Sarah off.

"Mother, you know that John—" she burst out, but stopped abruptly, gaping at John. He had snatched her sandwich and was stuffing it into his mouth in an attempt to startle her into silence. "Ouch," she cried as Harry's elbow landed belatedly in her side.

"But John," Mrs. Chase admonished him, "you certainly may have another sandwich. You must only let me know. What were you going to say, Sarah?"

"I forgot." Sarah blushed and John sat with his cheeks crimson.

"Perhaps dad left it in the shed. He was working on the crab nets." Harry took care not to look at John. He really went a long way to protect a secret. And he had been extremely quick.

They finished the meal in silence.

"Harry, will you mow the lawn. Sarah, will you clean up the kitchen. John, will you rake the cuttings."

Mrs. Chase said each sentence without raising her voice, John observed. She did not expect an answer, let alone an objection, and Sarah did not tell her it was his turn to do the dishes because he had lost the race into the water.

"Yes," mumbled Harry and Sarah.

"I'll be off to the market. I won't let you go hungry to Thatcher Island. Or does one of you want to come along? John?"

John shook his head. He had to get upstairs to fetch the knife, which he had forgotten and left in his other pants after trimming off the trouser legs of his jeans. When he entered the room, Harry was hovering over his suitcase.

Harry had come up to pick up his father's knife and plant it in the shed. But the knife was gone. He searched the shelf, the floor, under the rug, and behind the bed and was debating if he should comb through John's suitcase, when John came in. He looked up.

"The lawnmower and the rake are in the shed." He walked to the door and they went down together, watching each other.

Harry started the mower, mowing in very straight lines, taking sharp ninety-degree turns at the corners, the way his father liked it. If his father got angry at him after tomorrow, a neat lawn might persuade him that Harry was not all bad. He was also going to straighten his room, take the trash out without being asked, and clean up around the garbage cans.

John raked behind him. He liked the feel of the rake in his hand and the even strokes that were required to pile up the cut grass. And he liked the smell. If he had not found Harry lurking over his suitcase, he would have told him that Mr. Chase's knife was in his pocket. But Harry had insulted him with his suspicion.

When Harry was trimming between the roses, Sarah called him to the phone. He ran, expecting Doug's message about details.

It was his friend Mike, reminding him about tomorrow's scout project: They had planned to clean up Quamhassett Beach.

"I can't come," said Harry. "I have other plans." The project had slipped his mind completely, but he did not apologize.

"What plans?" Mike sounded as offended as Harry would have been in his place. "You knew about the clean-up!"

Harry put the receiver down. There wasn't anything he could say now. The phone rang again.

"Take your whaler to the eastern cove at eleven o'clock sharp." He heard Doug's voice at the other end of the line, brusque and commanding. "Any other questions?"

"Ye—yes," stammered Harry. "I mean no." All he could think of was that it was not "his" whaler.

"Great!" shouted Doug. "I knew we could depend on you!"

The line went dead.

And Harry, who a second ago had been ready to give up the game and Doug and Patrick and the team and his glorious day on Thatcher Island, because how could he take his father's boat?—he was hardly allowed to handle it with his father right at his side—rushed into the kitchen to look for the keys for the whaler. As usual, they were hanging on a nail above the schedules of tides and the sun and moon calendar.

He pocketed them.

Fifteen years after the hurricane of 1879, at the beginning of summer recess Davie Nickols, eleven years old, took his catboat to Thatcher Island. He landed not long after school closed, dragged the boat into the bushes and erased its tracks on the sand. For two days and two nights he scanned the waters from the top of Gull's Head, sleeping for short hours curled up in the grass, cutting his initials in any bark that would hold them. On the third day it started to rain; he had eaten his supplies; the fool-proof method of making fire with two sticks did not work; the raw fish tasted horrible. The search party picked him up in the afternoon. He was glad to see them.

"We'll go to the harbor," declared Harry a few minutes later. He had to know if the whaler was ready for use. He couldn't ask his father if there was enough gas, could he?

"Why now?" John had been going to enlist Sarah to help him repair her tree house. He had seen nails and tools—a hammer, a pair of pliers, a handsaw, drills, and screwdrivers—in the shed.

"To show you around!"

"Yes, the harbor," Sarah joined in. "You have to see it, John."

Harry pedaled ahead, yelling at them each time they lagged behind. But Sarah went on explaining a view or pointing out a rock or a flower. When Harry snapped at them again to hurry up, she told him to go on without them.

"We'll meet at the harbor," she said. "I'm showing John around."

Without another word Harry tore off.

"What's bugging him?" asked John.

"I guess he's seeing the Morrisons. They talked with him on the phone."

"And they'll kill him if he's late?"

They had reached the path to the dunes and Sarah turned into it. "Come on, John," she called. "You want to know where to dig cherrystones? It won't take long."

After a few yards they got off their bikes and walked into the marsh. The grass was sharp and pricked through the fabric of their jeans. Water soaked through their sneakers. They crossed a sandy flat.

The next flat was muddy and here they took off their sneakers. Sarah rolled up her pants and they sank ankle deep into the warm smelly grayish-black muck. It was fun to tread into it and they laughed as the ooze ran down their skin and squished between their toes.

Cherrystones? John thought. For a moment he pictured digging shiny red stones in the mud—precious stones—but that couldn't be true. He did not mind the smell any longer; he liked the feeling of slowly being sucked into the slosh, of stamping it, squashing it. What a beautiful marsh!

"Our marsh," Sarah had said, waving over miles and miles of outspread green land. It did not mean she owned it.

"We have to catch up with Harry or he'll be mad," sighed Sarah. "The clams have to wait."

They ran together over the spongy ground. Back at their bikes they broke into laughter. Sarah's face and arms and hands were covered with dark freckles, her T-shirt was speckled, and John too was splattered from head to toe.

"Marsh measles!" cried Sarah. "We've got marsh measles."

They followed the road. Now there were houses on both sides, and as the road curved gently, water became visible behind the ones on the left. It was one of those afternoons when the yellowish haze had finally crawled into the middle of the sky and swallowed up most of the blue. The sky had become closed and heavy.

"That's our harbor." Sarah gestured. She had wheeled into another left turn and stopped on a wooden platform above the water. Apparently landlocked, it lay quiet and shiny. Larger boats were moored serenely in its center; a number of smaller boats were tied to a lower dock. Someone was hoisting a sail and it flapped around the mast. There was hardly any wind and the sound carried over the water. Some kids were fishing from a dinghy. Otherwise they were alone.

John walked over to the edge of the dock and stared down. Here the water was almost black and bottomless. He spun around violently as someone touched him.

"I didn't mean to scare you," apologized Sarah. "I wasn't going to push you in. With your wound I wouldn't."

"I wasn't scared." John stepped back. It outraged him that he could not swim. Last summer at the public pool he had practiced without much success. He probably had not gone often enough, although he had not been afraid. "You have to put your head under water," Clarissa had said, and he had laughed at her and stuck his head into the water till she had pulled his hair, her face white and anxious. "Not that long! You'll drown!"

"Where's Harry?"

At that moment Harry was crouched in the whaler in

the middle of the harbor, checking the engine. The tank was full and should bring them to the island and back. Nevertheless he looked for the spare tank, though he knew that his father always stored it in the shed with the other gear. He liked being on the safe side. But there were only life preservers, a plastic pail, and part of a broken fishing rod. Too bad he could not start the engine and cruise through the harbor. Harry fingered the keys in his pocket.

With an enormous roar a motorboat appeared in the harbor, heading straight for the whaler. It changed direction in the last second. Doug waved, grinning, with Bruce and Wesley stern and sour-looking at his side. They swung into a circle; around and around they whirled, churning up the water. It boiled in their wake; waves crisscrossed the surface, tumbling over each other, taking the rowboat that had brought Harry out to the whaler along with them. A wave broke into the whaler and splashed Harry.

"Stop it!" he cried. "You're flooding my boat!" His voice was absorbed in the din of the motor and he was glad because it had sounded babyish. Anyway, Doug tired of the game after three more rounds and speeded toward the dock. His engine sputtered and died and the water became once more tranquil.

Sarah and John had watched the motorboat and noticed Harry in the whaler and his rowboat that was drifting away.

"I wonder what he's doing in the whaler," said Sarah. "Father says it's one of the basic rules to tie your boat securely and Harry hasn't done it. We'll have to help him get back."

Sarah and John were looking through the line of rowboats for one with oars as Doug Morrison and his companions docked, paying no attention to them. Doug strode ahead while Bruce and Wesley carried the gear to the upper dock.

"Don't look," whispered Sarah. "That's Doug Morrison. He's a friend of Harry's. We're going on the picnic with him to Thatcher Island."

"With him?" John frowned after Doug. He couldn't stand kids who needed a court of flunkies around them. Going on a picnic with Doug would probably mean being told what to do every minute.

"It's sort of complicated," Sarah tried to explain. "He doesn't know it yet."

"He's a friend of Harry's?" asked John. "Funny kind of a friend. I thought he was going to run him down! And he made him lose the rowboat. Look!" They saw Harry dive overboard.

Harry had struggled after the rowboat but it remained out of his reach. He had poked for it with the broken fishing pole, he had tried to catch it with a load of life preservers, hoping that one of their strings would loop around an oarlock so that he could pull the boat back—all in vain. Finally he decided to jump after it.

Something went wrong with the dive. Instead of slicing through the water he went almost straight down. The light became faint. For a second he felt the familiar heaviness, the numbness spreading through his whole body, and in a surge of panic he rebelled against it, fighting up to the surface. His body shook. He spouted water and with a couple of strokes recovered the boat. Then he rowed to the dock.

"Why did you go out on the whaler?" asked Sarah.

"No special reason."

They climbed to the upper dock. Doug squatted there, holding court with Bruce and Wesley in attendance. They were preparing his line, cutting bait, checking the reel while he tickled a puffer into monstrous size. "Funny how feeling important makes some people act all stupid," he said, as Harry approached. "Look at him! Doesn't he look ridiculous!" Doug rolled the rounded fish back and forth over the planks and with a final swat sent it over the edge. Bloated, it bounced off the surface of the water like a ball and disappeared out of sight under the dock.

"All set, Chase?"

Harry nodded. He couldn't very well talk in front of the others.

"Well, your boat is seaworthy. We made sure of that, didn't we?" Doug chuckled and Bruce and Wesley allowed themselves a brief grin. "We'll have some picnic!"

(78)

Several years after the Nickols incident, the Atlan-
tic Hotel Corporation leased Thatcher Island when
the mainland suddenly became popular as a resort
for the wealthy. The Corporation built a hotel and
a number of cottages on the mainland and put up
a tent, a beautiful and gigantic green and white
striped affair, in the western cove. The locals fixed
up their boats for rent, or they sailed and rowed
the well-paying guests over to the island for an
afternoon of swimming or a picnic, complete with
a band playing.

"I talked with Doug Morrison on the phone," said
Mrs. Chase. "Such well-brought-up boys, so polite and
friendly. They almost persuaded me to join you all
tomorrow."

Stiffly Harry waited at the door of the kitchen. They
had just come in after their ride to the harbor, and
Sarah and John had gone upstairs to wash off their spots.
He himself was still wet and quite cold and angry.

"It was gross what he did to the poor fish," John had
said earlier, and Sarah had agreed with him. He had
been speechless at the time. The sight of the bloated
puffer had been ugly and sinister.

"Yes?" Harry said to encourage his mother to go on.

"I was calling to find out when they planned to leave.
They said they'll pick you up at the harbor at nine-

thirty. I told them dad and I do have an earlier golf date. It was their suggestion that we drop you off at the dock. You wouldn't mind waiting. Probably not more than half an hour."

"Of course not," said Harry. He didn't mind waiting, he minded their easy camaraderie. Above all he minded that Doug Morrison and his mother were plotting what he had to do. As if they were going to push him into the game together.

"We'll get everything ready tonight," she said.

"We'll see," muttered Harry. Perhaps he could think of something to keep Sarah and John off Thatcher Island. Why should they come with him if they didn't care for his friends?

Mr. Chase helped them with their gear. He sent Harry and Sarah and John to bring sweaters or jackets, extra pants and shirts, swimming trunks and towels, and folded everything to be placed into a red duffel bag later. Nobody noticed that John did not pack a sweater for himself, but Harry displayed his Sunday pants and declared between bouts of laughter that John couldn't be serious about taking such fancy pants on a picnic to an uninhabited island. "You'll look pretty funny stalking around the island all dressed up for church," he cried, enjoying John's embarrassment. He was paying him back for what he had said about Doug.

"There's nothing wrong with them," said Sarah.

"Better take a tougher pair," advised Mrs. Chase.

Gritting his teeth, John went up to search through

his suitcase, though he knew perfectly well he did not have another pair of pants. When he came down again they had all left for the shed, where Mr. Chase selected rods and everything else needed for fishing. The pants were not mentioned again, but Harry now gave him a friendly grin.

"I hope you catch a big one, John!"

"You'll need the first-aid kit, matches, a flashlight." Mr. Chase went down his mental list.

"Why all that?" inquired Sarah. "We'll be back long before dark."

"Better be on the safe side," remarked her father lightly. He checked the flashlight himself and replaced the batteries. Then he told them he would have let them take his Swiss army knife, but he couldn't find it. "A knife like that is really useful," he said.

Harry looked at John, whose face showed nothing, but Harry thought he saw him patting his pocket.

"All set," declared Mr. Chase, tying the bag. "Except for the food. That's mother's department. You'll like the island, John."

John nodded. It was funny how they all assumed he would like the same things as they did. Some of the time he did, like eating fried chicken or zooming along on a bike, but he would much rather have worked at the tree house than go on a picnic with someone like Doug Morrison.

On his way to the kitchen, Harry touched the fishing rods and lifted the bag. It did not weigh much. Yet it disturbed him. It was so real, so ready to be carried to the whaler tomorrow. He put it down in the darkest corner.

"Something the matter?" asked John.

"Oh, I don't know," said Harry. "We won't need half the stuff. They never let you decide for yourself."

"Decide what? Don't you want to go?" Harry had talked of nothing but the island ever since he came.

"Sure I want to go." Harry pushed his doubts away and walked in on an argument between Sarah and Mrs. Chase.

"We are invited," insisted Sarah hotly, and she seemed to believe it herself now. "They'll be hurt if we prefer our own food. You said so yourself when we went over to Aunt Mary's."

"That was different," Harry put in quickly. "You always bring your share to a picnic."

He stopped Sarah's reply by stepping on her toes and watched as his mother assembled potato chips, apples, a loaf of white bread, and several cans of soft drinks on the table. He was relieved and at the same time troubled because he had taken another step.

"Harry is right," said Mrs. Chase, adding cookies, napkins, candy bars, and a honeydew melon. "Remind me to get out the hot dogs tomorrow. I'll leave them in the icebox overnight so they won't spoil."

"We won't need them. We'll grill our own fish," said Sarah grandly. "Too bad we didn't have time for the clams."

(82)

"If we catch any," murmured Harry.

"How about marshmallows?" asked Sarah. "It isn't a real picnic without marshmallows." But they were out of them.

"Is there anything special you would like to take along, John?" Mrs. Chase smiled at him. "What does your mother prepare for a picnic?"

John squirmed.

"Potato salad," he said finally because Mrs. Chase and Sarah were still waiting for an answer. "Potato salad and hamburgers and garlic soup."

"Garlic soup!" Sarah laughed.

"Not very practical to take along on a picnic," observed Mrs. Chase. "It's likely to spill. We couldn't afford a new hamper so often." She turned to fill the basket.

"But mother," said Harry, "how about a thermos? We always bring coffee in a thermos!"

After she had joined Mr. Chase in the living room, Harry unpacked everything. Somehow it made tomorrow less certain, made him still free to decide if he wanted to go at all.

"Did we forget something?" asked John. It was the first time he had said "we." Harry shook his head.

"You'll be in charge of the food," he said. "Sarah can't be trusted with the hamper. She'll eat the candy bars if we give her a chance."

"That's a big fat lie and you know it!" Sarah marched out of the kitchen. "Coming, John?" He left with her, and if Harry had wanted to confide in him, the time had passed.

They watched TV together till Mr. Chase sent them to bed early, saying something about a big day tomorrow and needing a good night's sleep.

"It's because he wants to watch a show we aren't supposed to watch," grumbled Sarah. "Something with a lot of blood and gore, real wild." She lingered in the boys' room.

"I'm taking a shovel," she announced.

"Then you have to carry it," said Harry ungraciously. He did not ask her why she wanted one. He could guess, though. She was going to look for Robert Thatcher's treasure just as he had told John she would.

"Perhaps we're not going. Perhaps we're staying here," he said. His voice quavered. Tomorrow loomed big and threatening and he still didn't know anything about the game. Sarah and John, too, were going to weigh him down. What if he did something wrong? He was going to be held responsible. Worst of all, he suddenly did not know if he would measure up to Doug's expectations.

"But we can't," protested Sarah. "Everything is arranged. The Morrisons invited us. Mother and dad know about it. Their day is all set. You told Mike and the scouts off. Our gear is ready, the food and the extra clothes. And you should have seen Marilyn's face when she heard about it! Besides, John and I want to go."

Harry knew she was right. It was too late to get out now.

"Couldn't we get lost on the way over?" asked John, but Harry couldn't tell if he cared one way or the other.

"Not with Doug and Patrick," cried Sarah. "They won a trophy."

"For wrestling," commented Harry.

"We could picnic in the dunes, couldn't we?" said John. If Harry was serious about changing his mind and not going, John thought, he needed some sort of trick to get out of his net of commitments—like losing the way or faking a sprained ankle. Simply saying no now required too much strength. John was willing to help him. The more he thought about the swollen fish, the less he liked the Morrisons.

"Everything will be all right," Harry said, to comfort himself.

PART
3

In the middle of the second summer of the hotel operation, Thatcher Island was shrouded in fog for a number of days. Nevertheless the band rowed over and played every afternoon, till on the fifth day it was carried with its boat far out into the open sea. The drummer had figured the tides incorrectly. A fog bank swallowed the boat. When Elias Fish and his crew—some thirty miles south of Carver Lighthouse—ran into a musical fog that trumpeted "Nearer My God to Thee" over the water, they were sure their last hour had arrived. Loud and very human cursing made them realize their error and they began rescue operations. The band was saved, but the tent was taken down and the rides to the island discontinued.

The morning came with cool soft gray fog, which soaked up the bright colors of the days before and muffled each sound.

"Don't you worry, John. The fog will be burned off by noon," said Mr. Chase as they loaded the car. They had all slept late and now were in a hurry to get started. Harry ordered Sarah and John around. He was eager and excited, his doubt gone with the night.

"The hamper, John! Sarah, the rods! And you carry the bag too! Put it here, not under the golf bags, you idiot. You'll squash the bread!"

"It's a specially hot day in New York." Mr. Chase smiled. "You chose a fine time to visit with us, John." He drove out on the road and past the meadows and woods and marshland. They stopped at the dock.

"Well, kids, you better get out. Sorry, but dad and I have got to leave. Golf first and then Boston. We may be late." Mrs. Chase helped them unload their stuff. There was nobody else around and the water was gray and smooth, its boundary dissolved in the fog.

"Have a marvelous time and take good care of John," Mr. and Mrs. Chase called as they backed out. "Don't forget to wear life preservers aboard. The Morrisons will be here in a little while."

"We'll be fine," promised Sarah.

"We'll have a great time," Harry assured them.

John waved after them. If Mr. Chase had to talk about the heat in New York, he thought, it was probably because he could not think of anything else that might interest John. He did it to be friendly.

Harry was dangling the keys in front of Sarah and John. "We're taking the whaler to Thatcher Island."

"But Harry . . ." Sarah began doubtfully.

"Didn't you hear dad talk about life preservers and taking good care of the boat?"

"But . . ." Sarah began again.

"Come on!" Harry picked up the rods and skipped to the lower dock. Here he climbed into their rowboat. They followed him with the gear. Harry supervised the loading and supervised the rowing and told Sarah to copy John's stroke—he was pushing his oar through the water with the right amount of force.

John was pleased. He liked handling the oar and enjoyed moving it through the water just below the surface. He had hardly ever done it before and he was doing it right.

When they reached the whaler, Harry scrambled across, ordering Sarah to tie up the boat and John to hand him the gear. Then he was busy at the engine. Harry acted as if he knew what he was doing, and if his hand shook a little and he had trouble fitting the key into the slot, it was only because it was exciting to be in charge alone. He should have been allowed to handle the whaler alone long ago. Everybody his age was.

"Funny I didn't hear you and dad talk about the whaler. I bet it took a long time to persuade him." Sarah stood near him.

"Yeah." Harry was very vague.

Just then the engine roared.

"Put on the life preservers," called Sarah.

Harry grinned at her and John, full of pleasure. They were tearing through the harbor. Sarah and John held on to the sides.

The boat headed for the channel. Harry began to sweat. It was a narrow passage, perhaps a hundred feet long and twenty feet wide, lined with ragged gray rocks. As he aimed directly for it, he forced his hands not to tremble. John beside him closed his eyes as if this were a way to avoid a crash. Suddenly he was heaved up and dropped painfully on the fishing rods. Again he was lifted and dropped.

"Here we go!" shouted Harry. John blinked at the big waves that were struggling to squeeze through the confined space, pushing and climbing on top of each other, spilling over rocks and swelling huge again. Ahead were more waves, a whole ocean full of them. Sarah grinned, saying something he couldn't hear, but seeing her at ease reassured him. At last they gained the open sea. Harry wiped his face and turned the motor full speed. So they shot along, flying above the water, touching its steely surface in quick violent beats.

It was beautiful.

It was beautiful the way the wind whipped their faces and tugged at their clothing. The speed took their breath away; their bodies danced with the rhythm of the boat. How far they traveled in such a short time!

Already the entrance to the harbor had faded into the band of curled-up fog that marked the shoreline.

Harry cut off the engine and the whaler bounced to an unstable halt. "Look at all the lobster pots!" he shouted into the silence, pointing to a number of white cubes that bobbed on the water. "Have you ever raided one, John?"

John did not answer. Sure, he knew what a lobster was. He had seen pictures of it, and a couple of dead ones in a store window. But he had never plucked one from the water, if that was the way you got them. The boat rocked uncomfortably.

"Yes!" cried Sarah. "A lobster for the picnic!"

Harry made sure that there was no other boat in sight. Raiding lobster pots is illegal and he didn't want to be caught. But they had plenty of time before meeting the Morrisons. Moreover it was a point in his favor to show up with a couple of lobsters. So he reached for the nearest cube and hauled aboard the line that was fastened to it.

"Nothing," he said, and John caught a glimpse of something very much like an orange crate two feet below in the water before Harry let the line sink back.

"That one over there!" urged Sarah. It proved empty too.

Harry flipped the motor on and steered the whaler into another group of markers. "Better luck this time!" Again he drew in the line.

"It's a big one! You wouldn't believe how big it is!"

he yelled. Sarah helped him drag the crate on board. It was about three feet long and a little over a foot wide and deep, made of wooden slats with spaces between each slat. Something moved inside.

Harry stuck his hand through some sort of netting, grabbed the animal, pulled it out and held it up. John stepped back as far as possible. He saw a mass of limbs, jerking in abrupt uncoordinated movements. And claws! Terrible claws. Reddish brown and big and dangerous. It took him a while to distinguish eight legs, the antennae, and two claws and to realize that the lobster was quite helpless in the air. It was not actually attacking Harry, merely fumbling with all its limbs.

"Can I have him?" he asked. The lobster was just the right thing to bring back home to Walter, who had wanted something wild like a tiger or a snake. As if the countryside were crowded with beasts.

"It will die without water," said Sarah. "Anyway we were going to eat it for lunch."

"I'll put him in a pail. I could take him home on the bus. We do stop at a gas station where I can get fresh water for him. Can I have him?" He would never ask for himself but for Walter it was different. Walter did not ask for many things.

"Lobsters need salt water," remarked Harry.

"I'll pack some." John was determined to keep him.

"You need ocean water. It has the right amount of salt," lectured Harry. "But even with sea water it would not survive in a small pail for lack of oxygen."

(94)

"You could pack it in ice and seaweed like the dealers do," said Sarah kindly. "Couldn't we do that, Harry? But I don't understand what you want with a lobster."

Before John could tell her that he wanted him as a pet for his brother Walter, Harry observed: "He wants to eat it. What else can you do with a lobster? Boil it in a large pot, watch its color change to red, and whack its tail and claws open when it's done."

He regarded his prisoner clinically.

"This guy is big enough for four people. We'll need it today. We'll catch one later for you."

"Forget it." John turned away. It had been stupid to set his heart upon a lobster and even more stupid to plead for it. He did not want anything from the Chase family; he never had.

Harry stuffed the lobster into the pail. Its legs rasped against the plastic. It was going to come in handy to placate Doug and Patrick. He could always catch another one for John.

The whaler jumped forward again. They were heading east, keeping the same distance from the coast, which formed a thick gray band between the delicately veiled sky and the steel of the water. Another heavy line appeared ahead of them. It gradually broadened as they approached and broke into various shapes and colors. Round, pointed, high, low. The white of the beaches, the many-hued greens of the plants, the dark of the rocks, all washed with gray.

"That's Thatcher Island." Sarah moved close to

John. "Doesn't it look eerie the way it creeps out of the fog?" She hugged herself, life vest and all. John, too, shivered with sudden cold.

⚜

Myles Bouchard had seen Thatcher Island creeping out of the fog as he sailed past it, following the bluefish year after year in September. That's how he painted it: Gull's Head, dull in a dull sky. The eastern cove with the fog rolling in. The western cove almost dissolved in the water. The long stretch toward Baker's Point, steaming after a rain. Gull's Head shrouded, bleak, exposed. But since in his paintings he called it "Northern Island," Thatcher Island did not become famous.

Nervously Harry fussed over the controls and wished the first meeting with Doug and Patrick and the others would be over, although he knew how he would account for Sarah and John. "You know, I couldn't help bringing them. I was left in charge at the last moment," he rehearsed for himself. "Sarah won't bother us and John is really tough. We can use him."

He steered closer to the shore and then turned the whaler south. He meant to circle Gull's Head to reach the eastern cove. It gave him a chance to try to locate any other boats anchored in either cove or at the foot of

Gull's Head. Maybe he wasn't the only one arriving early. But as much as he searched, he could not make out any sign of life, on the beaches or the land or the water. The eastern cove seemed empty too.

"The Morrisons said to meet here," he shouted over the noise of the engine, taking the whaler into the oval of much quieter water. Then he turned the motor off. "Anchor!"

Sarah let the anchor down. They were perhaps fifty yards away from the shore and the boat swayed gently.

"Why way out here?" asked John. It meant starting the day on the island wet from the waist down.

"It's a shallow cove with a lot of boulders," Harry told him. "Dad wouldn't like it if we scraped the bottom."

"Or got shipwrecked," added Sarah.

"We'll wait here." Tense, Harry faced the open sea, looking for Doug and Patrick Morrison. Too bad he didn't have any information about the other team. He would have liked to report a boat almost concealed behind a pile of rocks at the foot of Gull's Head or the movement of people in the bushes of the western cove. Sarah yawned.

John bent over the pail and inspected the lobster. The pail was small and the lobster had been crammed into it head first. Now it could not turn around, stretch, or free itself. Its legs twitched, its antennae quivered, its body jerked. John wanted to pick it up, shift it around, make it more comfortable, but when he touched the hard shell, one claw opened and his hand shrank back.

The claws were enormous.

Sarah passed him a plastic cup and he began to ladle water over the beast. He ladled till he had filled the pail, but the lobster did not appear happier. It was still imprisoned. John frowned down at it, picked up the pail, and dumped the lobster overboard.

There was a big splash.

"Stop it, Sarah," Harry barked. He did not look over his shoulder. Sarah smiled at John and he grinned back at her.

"But it's boring," she said. "Why can't we go to the island?"

"Because we'll wait here."

"That's no reason. It's stupid."

"Okay, okay." Harry gave in. "You and John go ahead." It wasn't how he had planned it, but how could he stand waiting with Sarah nagging constantly? Besides, it might be better to meet them alone.

John and Sarah took the life preservers off. Harry handed her the duffel bag as she slipped overboard into the waist-deep water.

"My shovel!" They had left it in the car.

John followed. There was no word about his wound and wouldn't it hurt to get into the water. He was loaded with the hamper and the pail.

"I'll bring the rest," Harry called after them as they waded ashore, giggling together because he had not yet discovered that the lobster was gone.

"Boy, he'll be mad when he finds out." Sarah walked faster. Here the water came up to their thighs. It was clear and John saw the rippled sand and an occasional rock, with a band of seaweed waving with the current. The shadow of a fish flitted past.

As he stepped ashore his feet felt heavy with the water-filled sneakers. He should have taken them off before leaving the boat. They would not be dry all day.

"We'll set up camp here." Sarah dropped the duffel bag and stretched herself. John placed the hamper carefully on the sand.

Suddenly there was screaming all around and they were ringed by a group of big kids. They looked funny to John—dressed up and disguised as if they were playing natives, with paint-streaked faces and blackened T-shirts. Their hair was powdered with ashes and all of them wielded weapons: clubs, spears, sticks, ropes. Sarah too showed no sign of being scared of the group.

"What are you doing on the island?" they shouted down at Sarah and John from all sides. John counted them. There were eight and all of them huge.

"None of your business," said Sarah, and pressed her lips together. "It's not your island—or is it?" She took a step forward but the circle did not open.

"You tell us!" A kid, yellow-and-blue-faced with an enormously broad chest, poked without warning into John's ribs.

"You heard her," said John, though the punch took his breath away. He had not been prepared for anything that vicious.

The kid poked harder.

"We are with the Morrisons," gasped John.

"Louder!" demanded the kid and poked again.

"We are with the Morrisons," said John, and the group burst into laughter and began their horrible dancing. They leaped around, shoving and slapping each other, shrieking, and John was certain that the island was theirs.

"What is with the Morrisons?" Sarah looked puzzled. John wanted to tell her to keep quiet, to act indifferent, not to arouse them. Clearly they were on a hunt together, although he did not know what they were after. Like the guys down the block who assembled in noisy packs and suddenly started moving, becoming dangerous. But he was standing too far away from her.

"You hear her, Rhino?" The smallest of the bunch boxed the big kid's belly.

"You hear her? How dumb Jumbo thinks we are?"

"What is with the Morrisons?" Rhino mimicked her.

"They are here! They are here!" the horde shouted, prancing around.

"Where are Doug and Patrick?" Sarah leaped at one of the group. He launched her playfully. She was caught by another boy and tossed back, pushed again and like a ball passed along their circle. It looked like fun, but it scared Sarah. John saw the tears she tried to hold back roll down a face stiff with fear. At his first movement to help her an arm tightened around his neck. He smelled the ash.

Sarah was very quiet when they let her go but she protested once more as they started wrecking their gear. "What are you doing?" she cried. "Stop it! Stop it!"

One of them slapped her hard across the mouth. She threw herself upon him, clawing and biting and kicking. They needed four of their group to pull Sarah away and subdue her.

And they were rough.

John had watched the ruin of his Sunday pants with some pleasure. They had ripped them in two. "Lost at sea" was a perfect explanation for the missing pants, as well as for the sweater he did not own. He had been totally helpless to protect Sarah. At the slightest move the arm around his neck had strangled him.

"No, no," he croaked as they tied her hands and gagged and taped her mouth while she strained against their hold.

"Gordon, shut him up too," grunted Rhino.

Gordon apparently liked the job, strapping John's arms inside his shirt and pasting the tape across his mouth. He did it meticulously and cruelly. John offered no resistance. He could not fight eight of them, but he filed away their faces, visible under the paint, their contours, gestures, voices. He blinked at Sarah, a signal of encouragement, and she held her chin higher.

"We'll dump them in the pit," Rhino said, and his companions guffawed. "To celebrate the opening of the games!" Then they pushed and dragged their prisoners up the beach into the bushes.

John did not look around for Harry. He must have watched it all. He would know what to do. It was his island, the way he had talked about it. And he must have suspected that something queer was going on; he had been worried yesterday evening as he unpacked their gear. What had happened to the Morrisons?

Myles Bouchard's notebooks scattered over the years contained a number of quick sketches he called "invasion." Only someone familiar with Thatcher Island would have recognized its outline. It was transformed into a naked rock swarming with birds. An island fortress attacked by warships. A garden assaulted by strange insects. A dead seal crawling with worms.

Harry was studying the entrance to the cove and the water beyond, though it was still early. The screaming and shouting came as a shock. As he swiveled around he saw several figures break through the bushes at the southern edge of the cove and run across the sand toward Sarah and John, who only now had reached the shore.

So the Morrisons had planned a surprise!

But it was an odd form of greeting, somehow disturbing. Harry cowered deep into the whaler, peering over the rim. He counted about ten figures, the smaller ones, Sarah and John, at the center of a circle, while the larger ones danced around them. From his post he could not make out who they were as they whirled around. They looked alien.

On they danced, pushing and shoving each other, tumbling down and rolling in the sand, till something made them crane their heads toward the water. Harry ducked down and lay flat on the fishing rods, listening to a renewed outburst of screaming laughter. He waited a long time before he looked again. The beach was deserted.

Harry groaned.

So they were going to surprise him too.

As if he didn't know they were waiting for him. They expected him to play their game. Warily he lowered himself into the water. Today he hated the wetness that soaked through his sneakers and filled them, crawled up into his pants and around his legs and body. He looked for the pail with the lobster, but it was gone. John must have carried it ashore. Now he had to come empty-handed. He trembled and for a moment held on to the boat. Then he let go and walked steadily toward the island.

"I'm coming, I'm coming," he chanted. Now they knew about Sarah and John. There was nothing he could do.

The beach, rocky and steep toward Gull's Head, broadened and filled with sand where it hugged the cove. It rose gently, became overgrown with beach grass, and disappeared under a cover of scraggly bushes. There were piles of grayish-white wood on the beach, planks and boards and strangely shaped roots and branches, multicolored plastic containers, foam rubber, dark masses of seaweed and kelp; but none of these piles was high enough to conceal the group. They must be hiding in the bushes. Harry waited for something to happen.

He stood at the edge of the water, dripping wet, uncomfortable, his sneakers squishing when he moved his toes, his heart beating loudly in his chest, waiting to be pounced on. He felt all their eyes on him and he shuddered.

Why did they let him wait so long?

He was on their team, wasn't he?

What kind of a game was it, anyway?

Then he saw a dead sheep, its wide and vacant eyes staring straight at him. Harry laughed uneasily. Here he stood just like another sheep, dumb and docile, waiting to be pushed around.

Bracing his shoulders, he turned his back to the beach and counted. First up to ten. He added another ten and another ten. When he finally allowed himself to glance back, nothing had changed. There was the sand, the wood, the debris, the dead animal.

They had not returned.

"Sarah, Sarah!" he called. His heart kept beating in his throat, right under his tongue, and his call was muffled. Harry forced himself to shout.

"Sarah! John! Sarah!"

Sarah and John heard him call.

They were not very far, roped to Rhino, who, after a whispered conference with his companions, was towing them inland by himself. Still, there was no hope of escape. Rhino was as powerful as a truck. Sarah and John stumbled after him and he jeered each time one of them tumbled over a root, or a branch whipped their faces.

"Who's that?" Rhino raised his head. "Well, the others will take care of him. He isn't calling you, is he?"

Sarah shook her head.

"Or you?"

John shook his head too.

Rhino grinned and sent John tottering into a path of shiny green and yellow leaves. He yanked the rope and John fell down.

"Poison ivy," he chuckled. "A little something to remember us."

John scrambled up quickly, trying to stay out of Rhino's way. But he had no chance. Once more he was thrown into the poison ivy.

"Not so quick," muttered Rhino. It was clear that he was angered by any sign of defiance, as earlier he and the others had been roused by Sarah's rebellion. But John and Sarah were by no means safe as long as they were obedient. Rhino liked to see them miserable.

John sighed. At least he knew that Harry was still free.

Their wanderings ended in a small clearing. Rhino prodded them into its middle and cut the rope, nudging them forward. Sarah and John were forced to jump into a hole. Six feet, seven feet deep. A wonder they didn't break their bones, John thought.

"Want a Coke?" Rhino asked from above. Sarah nodded, thinking that his horrible game must be over. He opened a can, sprinkling the sticky liquid over them. Sarah stood motionless in the middle of the pit, blinking up at him while it rained down on her. She tried to look scornful. John squeezed against the wall. He had long ago decided to be more economic with dramatic gestures. They wasted energy.

"See you later!" Rhino covered the opening with branches and walked off, laughing.

Sarah paced in the semidarkness and John counted her steps. Seven steps across and seven steps back or a circle of twenty-one steps along the walls of their prison. Then he examined the walls. They were constructed of big boulders with crevices between them. Not difficult to scale if you could use your hands. He started to rub his arms against the roughest corner he could find. It was going to take hours to wear the fabric down, but he was not going to depend entirely on Harry.

Harry had slumped into the sand. The sun was burning through the fog just as his father had said it would, thinning it before destroying whole areas. Small waves ran up the shore, pushing bits of seaweed along, moving tiny rocks and grains of sand. Harry tossed a cork into the water and watched it being carried up and down. Then he took his sneakers off so the others would see how comfortable he was.

But he could not sit still for long. He was troubled. What a lousy start for a game. The joke of letting him wait at the beach was wearing rather thin. It hadn't been very good to begin with.

So he put his damp sneakers back on and surveyed his surroundings for any mark they might have left. There was nothing out of the ordinary except a few specks of bright color farther along the beach. Pieces of plastic, some sort of detergent bottle. Nevertheless he walked closer. Then he ran. Soon he came upon the wreckage.

He could hardly believe his eyes.

Here was their gear—everything his father and mother had so carefully assembled—ripped and scattered. Their extra clothing was strewn about, halfway in the water. John's Sunday pants torn in half, the bread stepped upon and kneaded into the sand, the melon smashed to bits on a rock. The pail turned over and the lobster gone.

As if a pack of animals had run wild.

It did not make sense.

Confused and furious, he searched the wall of bushes. Were they still waiting for him? But why the destruction? What was going on? There was a rustling sound, leaves fluttered, and as Harry watched, too startled to move, a family of birds, brown-flecked and plump, appeared, eyed him, and fled into cover. Harry moaned.

"What's your hurry?" he called after them weakly.

Thatcher Island had always belonged to the birds. There were the "locals," who made their living year round, like the gulls and certain ducks and terns and plovers, woodpeckers and chickadees. Others came to breed, like the Great Gray heron, or to spend the summer, as some geese liked to do.

Twice a year great flocks of migrating birds paused on the island for food and rest. Men and women with field glasses invaded it at the same time to watch and count them. Once they had spotted a Gray Sea Eagle who had made the journey from Europe by mistake. There was something to celebrate at the Parson's Elm that night.

Harry poked around the remains of their gear. He tried a mouthful of bread but spat it out. It was like eating pure sand. One apple was still edible. Someone had taken the hot dogs, the soft drinks, the lobster, and the candy bars. His best find was the first-aid kit and a dry book of matches at the bottom of the duffel bag. He pocketed them both.

John wouldn't mind his Sunday pants ruined, he thought. They had warned him, hadn't they? So, he had brought them along to get rid of them. He didn't blame him. Who doesn't hate that type of shiny pants? As he draped the other clothing over the wood to dry, he felt something hard and oblong in the pocket of John's swimming trunks. His father's Swiss army knife. So he had been right. John had swiped it.

But the whole mess here was absurd.

Or was it?

Suppose it had been the other team that had come screaming out of hiding to surround Sarah and John and take them prisoner? In a game of war it made sense. That's why he hadn't recognized anybody! Stupid not to have thought of it before.

Suddenly alarmed, Harry withdrew behind a mound of kelp. Flies buzzed around him. The kelp stank, or was it a fish, decaying inside? He studied the bushes till he was almost sure nobody was watching him. They had led Sarah and John away. They were being held prisoner somewhere and they knew nothing about the game. He had never explained it. That's why they didn't try to defend themselves! Even against eight John would have put up a fight. It was all his fault. He should never have let them go ahead alone. Now he had to try to find them. He was worried about Sarah.

Or should he wait for his own team?

The cove was empty except for the whaler and there wasn't another boat in sight on the sea beyond. Perhaps it had been a misunderstanding and they had anchored in the western cove. He had to go on alone or lose time. Harry had no trouble trailing them. They had not attempted to hide their tracks and blot them out. They had walked straight from the wreckage into the bushes. Once into the thick growth he found it a lot harder to tell what direction they had chosen. He needed his special scout training to read the signs: part of a footprint on a sandy spot, a broken twig, grass bent down. So his progress was slow.

Briers and vines snatched at his clothing. Here he discovered more evidence: hairs, the white thread from a T-shirt, a piece of woolen yarn that must have come from Sarah's sweater. Bluish-green.

Burrs clawed at Harry's shirt, scratched his skin. He paused often, listening to the sounds around him, straining to hear voices, bodies pressing through the undergrowth, birds disturbed by some movement below. But there was only the breeze in the bushes, stirring the leaves, a small animal running, wood crackling in the midday sun.

When a branch snapped behind him, he stood frozen, taking a very long time to turn his head. Naturally, there was nothing but a curtain of unfriendly green. What did he expect?

When he reached higher ground, he had to retrace his steps again and again to pick up their trail. It was fainter, as if fewer persons had shaped it. The ground was rough and covered with rocks and short tough grass that did not hold an imprint. A narrow path wound around clumps of bushes, weaving in and out of similar tracks. Following their bends and curves, he soon lost his bearings.

He must have become reckless. When he bounded back for another check, he did not make sure that he was alone. They surprised him as he rounded a low thicket. Before he could see anything but a vague movement to the left behind him, Harry was thrown to the ground and pinned face down by a number of feet. Then they rolled him over with the tips of their shoes. Sneakers and boots. They were not particularly careful and he winced with pain.

"Who's that?"

"Dunno."

"Must have seen him around."

Two wet sneakers cradled Harry's head. A stick was placed on his throat, forcing his chin upward so that he stared into the upside-down face of its owner.

"Who are you?" He and the two others were a lot bigger than Harry. Their skin was smeared with black, red, blue, and yellow paint. Their hair was coated with soot or ashes. They looked wild and Harry could not make out who they were.

"Harry Wheeler Chase," he answered, just like on

TV. You are supposed to give your name and number, only he couldn't remember his Social Security number. Something with 27 in it.

"What are you doing here?" The tall skinny red-faced boy on his left accompanied his question with a kick.

"Ouch!" They must be from the other team. He had encountered the enemy!

"Answer!" Another kick.

"Fishing," said Harry dully. He was not going to give up yet, although it hurt so much more than he would have thought.

"Shall we tie him up and leave him?"

"We'll bring him to Doug."

Not Doug Morrison! *This was his own team then!* There was something so terribly humiliating in being captured by your own team, to be dragged before the others, to be ridiculed forever, that Harry wanted to die. It was all so incredibly unfair. He had done everything they wanted.

Harry felt betrayed. He had been told nothing about the game. He had not been marked as one of the team. He had no idea what was going on and where their headquarters were. What a fool he had been, never to ask any questions! What a slobbering, bootlicking fool!

He would not let it happen.

"We'll throw him into the pit with the others. Gordon can take him."

"Never!" shouted Harry, leaping up and tearing

through the bushes. He did not have much of a chance against three of them, but his unexpected move gave him a slight edge. Now they stampeded after him.

Harry kept to higher ground, darting in and out of the various tracks, twisting around clumps of vegetation and crashing through walls of green. When lack of breath forced him to stop running, he stood facing the path, ready to jump the first one who came upon him. He was not going to surrender without a fight. So he waited, unable to hear anything above the air rushing in and out of his lungs, watching for them to draw near. A dark mass pushed through the growth farther along the path. Harry clenched his fists behind his back and wished for a weapon.

When something wet and cool touched his hands, the shock was enormous. His heart exploded in his throat. Paralyzed, he felt a soft snout nudge him, breathe moist warm air over the skin of his arm, and prod his back. Again the snout searched for his hands.

"Help!" he screamed, and plunged forward blindly with no other idea in his head than to get away from whatever threatened him from behind. That he would be fleeing right into the arms of his pursuers did not cross his mind.

"Help!" Harry collided with a soft white and gray object.

"Bah baah baah bah," it complained.

"Bah baah bah baah baah," brayed a chorus of voices.

"Sheep," whispered Harry, pressing his face into the

wool. A large flock of sheep was trekking along each narrow path on their way to another grazing ground. They brushed past him, intent on their search for food, cramming the space between the bushes.

"What's all the noise?" That was Doug speaking on the far side of the herd. "Who are you after?"

Harry lay motionless among the sheep.

"Some little bastard."

"Rhino tells me they caught two of Jumbo's spies at the beach. Does he belong to them?"

"He didn't say nothing!"

"You didn't ask him?"

"There wasn't time."

"Well, what are you waiting for now? Get him!"

"Damn those sheep. They won't let us through."

"Sheep!" Doug's laughter mocked them. "Scared of sheep! Get the others to help you. Gordon or Patrick. Sheep!"

Harry crept down into the thick undergrowth, closer to the water. It was almost comfortable in his green den.

Five years ago the owners of Salt Meadow Farm rented Thatcher Island for summer grazing. They ferried the sheep over in May, freshly shorn and with their newborn lambs, and came to retrieve the flock after the first frost in November. During

the summer months the sheep took care of them-
selves. They raised their young, grew their wool,
and, if one of them died, death came naturally.
There was plenty of food and ample water at
Robert Thatcher's basin in the sweet-water swamp.
Besides, the farm people had built a simple shelter
against storms and heavy rains near Baker's Point.
It was a profitable arrangement for the people from
Salt Meadow Farm and they wanted to keep it.

It was hardly comfortable for Sarah and John. Their
situation had not changed. They were still tied up, John
with his own shirt used as a straitjacket, Sarah with her
hands bound tight behind her back. Their mouths were
taped shut. The skin around the tape burned, and their
arms and shoulders ached.

For minutes at a time they leaned against the rocks,
pumping their shoulders up and down in the effort to
shred their bonds. To rest, John squatted on the floor
while Sarah paced restlessly the seven steps across and
seven steps back. She kicked the walls, snorted as loud
as she could, and stared into the branches. She did not
understand what had happened. What had she done to
get thrown into a hole, bound and gagged? At times
she felt as frightened as she did that awful moment down
at the beach when they had played ball with her. Then
she turned to John.

John tried to comfort her with soft grunts. He was
pretty miserable himself. His left side especially was

hurting from the violent poke in his ribs. Too bad he had carried Mr. Chase's Swiss army knife in his bathing trunks. Now it was lost with all their gear and with it the hope of freeing himself and Sarah quickly the moment he extricated one hand.

He went back to the wall and began furiously to scrape against it. He was sick and tired of being a pawn in an unknown game. Moreover, he did not want them to find him and Sarah when they returned. There was nothing good to expect from them.

Sarah touched him and pointed upward. Leaves fluttered, insects buzzed, a gull screamed.

Was it Harry? Was he close?

She and John grunted as loudly and as wildly as they could. Then they listened into the silence before they continued their work. It must be almost noon and their throats were dry.

Where was Harry? Why didn't he come?

Harry was creeping back to the spot where he had run into the sheep. It took all his courage and still his knees were shaking and his legs heavy and useless and composed of Jell-o. He had to haul them along.

He crept back because he had suddenly understood that the "others" caught at the beach and now thrown somewhere into a pit could only be Sarah and John. He had to rescue them because they happened to be evidence that identified him. He could not leave them in Doug and Patrick's hands without being exposed.

He thought of nothing else.

(116)

Single-minded, he crawled back, burrowing through the scraggly brush, fighting vines and briers and roots and branches. At the foot of Gull's Head he darted from clump to clump, pressing into the tough scratchy plants to wait and listen.

Harry was lucky. He heard the group long before they could spot him. In fact, Doug's voice warned him into absolute, icy immobility, screened by a wall of thick vegetation. Sumac, blueberries, poison ivy, honeysuckle, he registered.

"We'll catch him later. With Jumbo's team so late we've nothing better to do. He won't get far," Doug said with lazy confidence.

"If it wasn't for the sheep . . ." One of Harry's captors excused himself.

"He got away before the sheep, didn't he?" Doug hit back fast and sharp.

"Yeah." It sounded very reluctant.

"I guess we'll stroll back to the pit. Link up with Rhino and Patrick and the others." Again Doug spoke softly.

Now they trampled along a track. Harry breathed deeply and walked after them, feeling rather smug. They were going to lead him straight to the ominous pit. And it was a cinch to follow them. They made enough noise for him to stay well out of range, tagging along the base of Gull's Head to the point of the island where Robert Thatcher once had built his cabin. From the border of a small clearing Doug and the three others strode across the open space, fierce-looking in their war paint and ash-colored hair, carrying weapons. Clubs and sticks, ropes, pieces of pipe. Harry watched them with pride. They were his team.

"Patrick? Gordon? Rhino?"

There was no answer.

"We'll wait." Doug kicked aside the branches that were piled in the middle of the clearing. "How are our pigs? Comfy?"

Pigs?

Ducking behind a dead tree, Harry heard riotous grunting and squeaking. There had never been pigs on Thatcher Island—or had there?

"Let's have a little entertainment as long as we're here," suggested Doug. "Want to see them jump?"

"Yeah, why not."

"Sure!" They drew close around the opening.

Harry almost stood up behind his tree. He knew who was grunting. He knew the voice. It was Sarah's and the other must be John's. But why squeak and grunt? Why not shout and scream? Was it part of the game?

For a moment Harry felt the comb at his throat, the mousetrap on his hand. He saw his boat nearly swamped, the puffer floating, their gear wrecked. Each time someone had been scared and hurt and punished or laughed at. And each time he had excused it or pretended not to understand it or even laughed along because he had been so flattered by Doug's attention. The perfect sucker.

But they wouldn't hurt Sarah. Or John.

Sarah was just a little kid who knew nothing about the game. And John was a stranger. Jumbo's spies! That was ridiculous. Still, he shouldn't have let them go ashore alone. Not without telling them about the game. Unhappily, he crouched down again.

The grunting sounded even more angry.

Harry watched as Doug and his companions flung dirt into the pit, broken twigs, small rocks. Then they held a spitting contest.

"Three feet away from the rim," directed Doug. "And you down there, keep on your toes!"

"Two feet away is plenty," protested the others.

What a preposterous match for someone like Doug. Harry blushed for him. Sarah and John down in the pit were no opponents. They had no way to fight back, to defend themselves.

Still, it was funny how each of them tried to outspit the other. What retching, sucking, chewing, smacking to collect the spittle. They laughed, and Harry, too, grinned against his will. Doug won easily, spraying a mouthful of Coke on his victims.

"You cheated," they exclaimed but followed suit, spouting soft drinks. The ones his mother had packed. Hadn't they done enough? They should stop now. Harry hated them as they went on and on, gargling Coke and Sprite. If John had only kept the knife in his pocket! He felt for it.

Things got worse.

Now Doug was striking a match. He flipped the burning match inside the opening, leaning forward to observe it fall.

The grunting grew louder.

"They like it."

"Here comes another one," announced Doug politely, sending a second match flaming on its way down. He was applauded.

The grunting grew shriller.

Harry hunched behind his tree, appalled.

"See how they jump," intoned Doug, and the three others sang along, marking each new match with savage shrieks. Then one of them began to set a dry branch on fire. He waved his torch around.

"Throw it! Throw it!" they shouted.

"Light up the hole!" Doug stepped back to make room for him.

Harry acted. He groped for a rock; he hurled it straight at the guy with the torch, hitting him in the back. Surprised, the boy stumbled and let the flare drop.

"I was hit," he stammered. "Right in the back. Some-one hit me!" He rubbed his back.

Harry let a handful of small rocks rain on the bushes to his left.

"Hear that!" they told each other. "Someone is hiding over there."

"Couldn't be Jumbo and his team. It's still too early."

"The kid we caught before!"

"Let's get him!"

"This time we'll do it right," commanded Doug.

They fanned out into the bushes where the rocks had come down, just like a bunch of idiots who had never understood this trick on TV. On Doug's order! Behind their backs Harry flew across the clearing and dived into the pile of branches. He plummeted to the ground.

"I came to free you," he whispered a little grandly, blinking up from the floor. "But hide me! Sit on me! Hurry!"

He rolled against the wall. John and Sarah perched on top of him. It was not a moment too soon. They were returning.

"Another silly blunder," Doug remarked in his deceptively soft voice. "First the sheep, now the birds. Quite some record. Or do you really believe there was someone?"

"What about the rock that hit him?" he was challenged.

"What rock? Bullshit."

Nobody answered.

"I'll stay around here," said Doug. "Why don't you guys go over to Gifford's Cove?"

They heard fast retreating steps.

"No more amusement for now, piggies." The branches were spread evenly over the top of the hole. Then it was quiet.

Recently there had been a number of differences about Thatcher Island between the owners of Salt Meadow Farm and the Audubon Society. Both parties wanted the island for themselves, for their sheep or birds respectively. During a teach-in of the bird people and a sheep-in of the farm people (a demonstration of shearing, spinning, and weaving) a fight broke out that ended in the courts. Now both sides were appealing to Mrs. Garfield Thatcher, the owner of the island, for a decision.

"Boy, that was close," breathed Harry, crawling out from under Sarah and John. Now he saw why they did not scream or shout. Their mouths were sealed. A white square of plastic bridged their faces. And they were tied up in a way that must hurt.

"Those God damn sons of bitches."

They couldn't have rules for their game that allowed them to torture and burn and hurt. But he had watched them do it as if it were nothing out of the ordinary. They did not need rules.

He stared at Sarah and turned to John and looked at him, his arms helpless at his sides.

"Sarah, I didn't know . . ." The words stuck in his throat. He wanted to tell her that it wasn't his fault, that he had had no idea something so terrible was going to happen. But it wasn't true. There had been clues and he had simply wanted to be blind.

"Sarah . . ."

Sarah twisted round to show him the work in progress on her rope handcuffs. He did not understand her in the weak light. He thought she was reproaching him for her misery.

"John?" he begged. John nodded toward Sarah's back.

Now Harry was aware of the frayed rope that was knotted tightly around her hands. He swallowed. With his father's knife he slashed it, precise, his action controlled. He was no longer dazed.

Sarah moved her arms gingerly, rubbed her shoulders, wiped some of the spit off her face, touched the tape and grunted softly. Then she examined a burned spot on her right sneaker. There hadn't been time to be scared when it rained burning matches, but now her knees shook.

"Those God damn sons of bitches," whispered Harry, and his voice was cold and sharp. He sliced through the fabric to free John. "They wrecked your shirt. And they wrecked your Sunday pants. I'll kill them." He felt ice-cold with anger.

John rotated his shoulders and clenched and unclenched his fists. Saliva had dribbled down his cheek, and hair near his left temple was singed. The last minutes had been pretty bad, scurrying around the narrow prison trying to escape the fire. But he had protected Sarah and himself. Only when he saw the torch had he been truly frightened. Doug and his companions did not know when to stop. Curious, he watched Harry, who seemed calm and level-headed and at the same time beside himself.

"Now the tape," sobbed Harry. "It'll hurt like hell and you can't scream. Not the least little bit. Or we won't catch the bastards and pay them back." All he could think of was revenge.

Gently scratching, he loosened a corner of Sarah's tape. John had put an arm around her to steady her. He winked and with one swift move Harry tore it off. Sarah gasped. Tears shot into her eyes. Even in the dim light they could see the bright red circle around her mouth.

"Bastards."

Harry patted Sarah while John was working on his own face. He had waved Harry away. It was better to know the exact moment of the sharpest pain and prepare against it. Still, he barely smothered a cry. It did hurt like hell.

"I have something that might help." With trembling fingers Harry searched for the first-aid kit, useful after all. "Petroleum jelly."

He dabbed Sarah's skin, offering the tube to John, who coated the area around his mouth.

"Better?"

Sarah nodded. It smarted far too much to speak.

"It was Doug Morrison," she mouthed. "Why?"

"What's going on?" murmured John. "Who's Jumbo?"

"We'll get them!" hissed Harry. "He's still up there, I know it. We'll get him and pay him back."

He clawed at the walls.

"But I'd rather go home," murmured Sarah. "I'm thirsty."

"Me too," John added, supporting her.

Harry did not hear them. He turned around and his bright and intent eyes were fixed first on Sarah's and then on John's face.

"They can't treat me like that. We'll pay them back. They tortured you."

"A little," breathed Sarah, hardly moving her lips. They had been cruel, especially Rhino and Doug Morrison, and for a moment or two she had been afraid.

"You were hit and bound and gagged. They kicked you. They imprisoned you. They used water and fire torture. They were going to burn you alive," he went on, his voice monotonous.

"Poison ivy," added Sarah to his impressive list. Harry was right. They deserved to be taught a lesson.

"Poison ivy," repeated John. "That was more like an accident. I could have landed in a different bunch of plants." He was for leaving Thatcher Island immediately. Harry and Sarah and he were still outnumbered. Besides, he was parched.

"Let's take the whaler back to Egham," he said.

Harry looked past him. "I thought you were tough."

Sarah edged away from him.

"Forget it! We'll stay." John gave in. There was no choice. He could see Harry was in a state where he couldn't be reasoned with, entirely bent on his need for revenge. Nor could he be left behind alone. There was no knowing what he would do.

"Good. I'll go after Doug."

All John and Sarah knew as they hoisted Harry up into the branches was his promise to send Doug crashing down to them to be bound and gagged.

"Get the ropes ready," he said, and brushed away all questions of how he was going to lure Doug into the trap. "I'll depend on you."

"He's crazy," whispered Sarah as Harry wiggled through the cover. "He is really crazy. We must stop him. Help me up!"

"This is our place." John was looking around for ropes and was lashing short pieces together. "Maybe he'll trick Doug—we're his bait. If he's crazy we have to protect him."

Sarah grumbled; nevertheless she copied everything he did. Then they waited.

Thatcher Island, as most people agreed, needed protection. Against too many sheep, or in a few years

*it would be barren from overgrazing. Against too
many visitors with their debris, destruction, and
fires, or the birds would surely vanish. Against plans
like putting up summer cottages, hotels, building a
marina, a resort. Unprotected, Thatcher Island
would be used for a number of years and then
abandoned. Wasted.*

Harry was not crazy. He was furious. He was so
furious that he could think of nothing but justice for
everything that had gone wrong, and the one to deal it
out to was Doug Morrison. He was responsible, wasn't
he? Anyway, he was at hand.

Harry had spied him, or part of him, sprawled behind a boulder at the edge of the brush. Using his most
careful scout technique, he crossed the clearing and
moved in a circle close up to Doug. He paid no attention to his fast-beating heart. Only his dry throat
bothered him and he swallowed several times to get rid
of the stale taste. Then he stood upright and walked
out into the clearing.

"Hello, Doug," he called. "The others told me I'd
find you here. What's going on so far?"

Doug merely turned his head.

"Oh, it's you, Chase," he said. "It's about time you
showed up. Jumbo's team is late. Some last minute
foul-up. So, we wait."

"Too bad."

"You should be painted." Doug threw him a fragment of red chalk. "It's Gordon's idea. He's sort of artistic."

Harry quickly rubbed his face and arms. If his captors should come back, they would not recognize him right away. He strolled over the clearing toward the piled-up branches.

"Hey, man, watch it!" shouted Doug. "The pit!"

"Pit?" They were both loud enough for John and Sarah to understand almost every word. How clever of Harry to warn them.

"Pit! Prison!"

"You mean underneath the wood?" Harry sounded incredulous.

"Yeah, pretty neat, isn't it? Thatcher's cellar. Rhino stumbled into it last year. Too bad it was empty. No treasure, not even his skeleton."

"Too bad," repeated Harry. "It's like an African trap for big game."

"Yeah, that's what Rhino thought, too. To chase Jumbo's team across the clearing. Or let them chase after us and plop-plop-plop—they disappear." Doug chuckled.

"I like that," Harry said reverently.

"We caught two already," Doug went on. "Down at the beach. Jumbo sent spies ahead. Little kids. Thought they would get away, being little."

"Mind if I have a look?" Harry asked coolly.

"Sure, have a look at our piggies." Doug spoke with affection.

Harry pushed the cover away, knowing what he would see.

Two figures sprawled on the floor, motionless, on their backs, their bodies twisted, their heads crooked at an unnatural angle. A white piece of fabric glowed over their mouths and cheeks. John's eyes were closed, but Sarah stared up, wide-eyed and vacant and bold.

Harry cried out. It was a wild cry full of anguish, for what he saw drove home to him that Sarah and John had been hurt. And that it was his fault. He had dragged them to Thatcher Island. He had handed them over to Doug and his group. He had betrayed them.

The second scream brought Doug immediately to Harry's side.

"Oh, my God," he whispered, and drew back to escape. Harry's presence kept him from rushing into the bushes. So he circled the pit slowly, with Harry close upon him, and to get away from this frantic supervision he climbed down. Here he avoided looking into Sarah's face and bent over to listen to her heart.

That's when Harry jumped on his back from above, toppling him. He had waited impatiently for the exact moment. Doug lost his balance and crumbled on top of Sarah, who groaned.

"John! John!"

John had already thrown himself on Doug's legs, coiling a rope around them. He was excited. His trick had worked beautifully. Harry's cry had been almost too real. Together with him he now tied Doug's arms and hands and made sure that the knots were secure. Then Doug was bundled off Sarah.

"Gosh, he's heavy! I'm glad you got him off," she breathed noisily. "Your scream made me shiver, Harry. We were quite a sight, weren't we?"

"We sure were." John once more checked the bonds. "We'll leave him here. Boy, he won't like it when his friends find him." He pictured the scene: the great Doug Morrison locked up by Jumbo's kid spies.

Harry studied Doug.

"What's it all about, Chase?" Doug seemed more astonished than concerned. "Why the show? And the tie-up?"

"You'll have to pay," muttered Harry feverishly. "You'll have to pay." He stopped and searched through Doug's pockets till he found the tape. Doug lashed out at him with both legs. John saw the rope strain and hoped it would be strong enough. He breathed easier when the thrashing stopped, and he had tied another length of rope between arms and legs.

"Pay for what? Aren't you on my team?"

"Your team!" cried Harry, and his voice trembled. "What a God damn lousy team!"

"Well, you slobbered all over us to join, didn't you?" observed Doug, grinning. "Did everything. Remember?"

Harry slammed the tape on Doug's mouth, crisscrossing the bandage. He knew Doug was right and he

(130)

couldn't bear it. He hadn't been any different from Bruce or Wesley; he had jumped at a twitch of Doug's finger; he had jumped though he knew what bastards they were. Flattered nevertheless. How he hated himself and how he hated Doug! He shook violently.

It was Sarah who started the dance.

"John! Harry! Let's dance around him, like on the beach. An eye for an eye!" She waltzed ahead and they trailed her. As she went faster, they went faster, tripping and stumbling in the half light. All their movements became wild and boisterous. They twirled around, excited.

Doug seemed amused as they began, but when Sarah bowed and slapped his face twice, his eyes changed expression. His jaw clenched even though it could not have hurt much. He tried to swat them with his bound legs and brushed Harry.

"You son of a bitch," hissed Harry, and punched at him in a frenzy. He didn't care where he was hitting Doug. He just punched and punched till Sarah, who was whirling around with John, pushed him aside. Harry leaned against the rock, tense.

"That's for being tied up, hit and dragged through the brush!" Sarah hammered at Doug with her fists. This time there was nobody to pull her back and tame her. Her face was flushed, the red circle around her mouth afire.

"That's for the poison ivy," growled John, and kicked at the body on the ground. He kicked repeatedly although he would rather have rubbed Doug's face with the poisonous leaves. An eye for an eye, as Sarah had said. John thought that he would have to keep a long distance between himself and the pit when Doug was released. It wouldn't be healthy to stay around. But Harry was not finished yet.

"What next?" He was breathing hard. His chest felt constricted. "We'll do it exactly the way they did it." It seemed very logical to blot out everything that had been done to them with similar acts.

"What else did they do?"

"Coke!"

"Coke?"

"They sprayed us with it. But it wasn't him, not the first time," explained Sarah.

"Water and fire," Harry went on to himself, waving the matches about. "I found them at the bottom of the duffel bag." He struck a match and held it close to Doug's cheek. Doug must have felt the heat and his eyes turned glassy. He was lying very still.

"Feel the heat! Feel it!" cried Harry. "Scares you, doesn't it? But you didn't mind scaring them." He let the flame burn to the very end.

John and Sarah watched him, suddenly bewildered and then shocked. As he told them to get out of the pit, they all scrambled up the wall, relieved. It was easy now they could use their hands. How good to be up! They had been cooped up for hours, hadn't they?

What time was it? The sun stood straight above them, though it wasn't possible, was it? Doug looked unimportant and harmless from above.

"Good-bye," called Sarah, and dropped a handful of dirt on him.

"Now spit!" snapped Harry.

"When do you think they'll find him?" asked Sarah, ignoring Harry's order. "Shouldn't we take his tape off? It's so uncomfortable."

"He'll get help before we're safe," warned John. "We really can't."

"Spit!"

"I'm tired," declared Sarah. "And we're doing just the same as they did and we didn't like it. It was cruel and it wasn't even him most of the time. It makes me sick to my stomach." She inspected with disgust the smudges of paint from Doug's face on her hands, and when the connection became clear to her she flushed even more.

"Spit!"

"Come off it," said John. "It's no fun any more. Besides, you make enough noise to bring the rest of them back." It had been fun to tackle someone as big and powerful as Doug Morrison, beat him, and imprison him. Dancing around in triumph was all right, with a kick or a punch to repay some of the earlier abuse. But they had all been carried away. He had kicked more than he liked to think about. Now he felt queasy at the

(133)

sight of Doug. "It's enough now." John reached for Harry's arm. "Didn't he say they thought we were spying for Jumbo?"

"Mistaken identity," Sarah put in. She was pleased. "Imagine, John, you and me spies! Though that's no excuse. Not really. Come on, Harry, let's go home." She pulled at his shirt.

But there was no stopping him. Harry shook himself free. His face contorted with fury, he spat into the hole, retched, spat again, spluttered. Then he stood gesticulating wildly, gurgling about treachery, paying back, breaking rules, meanness, cruelty, stepping on people, pushing people around, vain, stupid suckers.

It was terrible to watch him raving.

"I hate you all," he shrieked, and now he lighted one match after the other and flung them down. "You can't treat me like dirt! You can't! You can't! I'll show you."

Sarah clung to him while John, after an initial effort to stop Harry, kept his eyes on the matches. He was prepared to climb back to put out any flames. Doug had rolled himself against the wall and John saw the white of his eyes gleam. So John didn't see the one match that landed in the pile of branches.

There was little smoke at first. Suddenly, with a puffing sound, part of the wooden heap exploded into fire, expanding rapidly and enveloping the whole pile. The three of them stared at the flames aghast.

"Fire," whispered Harry, trembling.

(134)

There had been small fires and big ones on Thatcher Island throughout its history. The old ones left their records deep in the ground between layers of top-soil: a stratum of gray or black between light-colored sands. They were all caused by lightning and were quite rare. Only with the more frequent visits of people did the rate of fires increase, and during the last years parts of the island were black-ened almost regularly. Only the area around the sweet-water swamp was safe. That was where the oldest and tallest trees grew.

"Fire," gasped Sarah.

"The knife," demanded John.

Harry shook his head. He was numbed.

"He'll burn alive. You don't want that."

Harry swallowed and passed him the knife without a word. As John jumped into the pit, a great bundle of flaming branches cascaded down at the other side and he disappeared into a cloud of ashes, embers, and smoke. Harry and Sarah drew in their breaths sharply, but before they could let out a scream, John and Doug Morrison were clambering up, covered with soot, coughing, yet unharmed.

Doug tore the tape off and flinched.

"No hard feelings, Chase." He spoke very clearly. "It was just a friendly game. Got a little rough perhaps, so we'll forget that. Nobody forced you to come, remember?"

"Some game!" Sarah glared at him.

"Friendly game, friendly people, friendly town," singsonged John sarcastically, rubbing his naked shoulders. His shirt was hanging around his waist in shreds. Harry straightened up and faced Doug.

They all understood that Doug was never going to talk about what had happened in the pit and that they better keep their mouths shut too. It was nothing to boast about. For any of them. Smoke billowed around them.

"I better get help." Doug nodded curtly and then galloped across the open space, slipping into the bush in the direction of Baker's Point.

"One little match," Sarah exclaimed, awed.

They stepped away from the pit. The fire was quite spectacular, though most of the flames were still confined to the pile of wood on the clearing. Sparks were shooting into the air in a column of smoke, only slightly bent by the soft breeze. Smaller flames were creeping through the grass.

"It could have been them who started it." Harry was licking his dry lips. His painted face looked even redder in the glow of the fire. "Not that it matters." He was utterly exhausted and wanted nothing better than to wander off. He knew the fire was dangerous. It had not rained for some time, and crawling through the brush, he had felt the parched ground. But he was too tired to care.

"John?" he begged, wary of his own decisions.

"We'll fight the fire," said John quickly, as if he had been waiting to be asked. He thought he knew how to go about it. He had seen it on TV, where even a dog like Lassie was adept at fighting fires. Also it felt good to know his friends looked up to him. Though he would never acknowledge it, he had wanted them to. "Everybody get sticks! We have to push the fire apart and then smother it."

He grabbed a sturdy branch and soon he and Harry were working side by side, raking, spreading, and pounding the brands. Sarah was trampling on embers. Now she retreated a bit. Despite her damp clothing she could feel the heat. And John wasn't wearing a shirt. He looked like one of the Morrison team—face, arms, and chest blackened, hair covered with ashes.

"Watch out," he cried, pushing her sideways and swiping a cinder off her hair with his bare hands. "It's dangerous. Don't you know that? You have to stay back farther!"

"I stay right where you are," insisted Sarah, and kept on snuffing out flames with her sneakers.

Harry wiped his eyes. It was only going to be a very small fire. They wouldn't need help. They had ripped the heap of branches apart just in time and the flames were diminishing.

"Look over there," groaned John.

A huge flame was shooting out of the bushes at the edge of the clearing, sparkling and bright. Smaller flames were surging over the plants, eating rapidly around the clearing, scorching tree trunks, devouring branches, licking at leaves, charring the green into dull gray. Smoke crawled ahead and lingered where the flames had finished. There were greedy sounds of slurping, sizzling, zinging, snapping, crackling. The smoke rose high into the sky, yielding to the wind.

Powerless, they shrank back.

"They'll see it from the fire tower," said Sarah. "They'll send the coast guard and the firemen."

"Everybody in town will know." Harry sounded quite hopeless.

"Will they send planes?" asked John. That's what happened on TV once when the fire raged out of control.

"I don't know." Sarah looked at the sky, which was blue and empty except for the smoke.

"What about the animals?"

"They'll be safe at the swamp."

The fire was circling the clearing. Hot, suffocating smoke rolled in from all sides. They started coughing.

"It's no use any more," said John, scowling. "It's bigger than us and we can't do anything. Pretty dangerous, too."

Harry turned his head slowly and took it all in: Sarah nervously tripping from one foot to the other. John

(138)

glaring at the fire, angry because it had outrun him. The blaze all around, the burned-out pit, the smudged sky, and beyond it Gull's Head and the coves and the long stretch to Baker's Point unscathed as yet. In a way he wanted to see it go up in flames, with all that had happened buried in the fire. But it wasn't the island that had gone wild. It was him, and the consequences were his to bear.

"We'll go back as fast as we can to inform the fire department in case they don't know." Harry's voice was firm but strained.

John had watched him thoughtfully. "You'll tell it all?" There was probably a lot more than he knew so far. He could guess that Harry had been a member of Doug's team, a very low member; that he had come to the island for the game, taken the whaler without his father's permission. And he had caused the fire. It was a lot to tell and would take courage.

Harry nodded. He felt calm and free.

"All right. Where do we go?"

"To our right! To the cove!"

They were running through the grass.

Before cutting across the clearing, Sarah crushed a last smoldering branch into the ground that burned through the sole of her sneaker and injured her foot. In the first excitement of flight it did not bother her much, but soon she straggled behind. Inspecting the foot, she found pinkish skin visible through the hole.

"Sarah, hurry, hurry!"

Bravely she limped along, turning the foot sideways, tiptoeing, hobbling every other step. A whiff of smoke caught up with her and made her pause to cough.

"Sarah, where are you?"

Harry and John found her almost in tears.

"My foot, it hurts so much! And my throat!"

"We're already there," Harry comforted her. It wasn't quite true but he had to encourage her. He couldn't let anything more happen to Sarah or John. Lagging behind was getting far too dangerous.

"If you put your arms around us?" Supporting her on both sides, they pulled her along. The noise of the fire was near and a new wave of smoke blew through the undergrowth. At last they gained on the fire, escaped from smoke and crackling sound. Breaking through the curtain of brush at the beach, they saw no boat other than the whaler. The sea glittered empty under the midday sun.

"Why isn't anybody here?"

"They can't miss that!"

The column of smoke behind them had broadened, fanned by the wind, and ranged high into the sky.

"Come on," cried Harry. "We have to get help. The island will burn and it's all my fault."

Sarah was limping swiftly toward the water. "It'll hurt, won't it?"

"I'll carry you." Harry picked her up.

"You go ahead and get the boat ready," said John. "I'll take Sarah."

He carried her piggyback. She weighed less than his sister Clarissa. As he went ahead into the water, Harry hastily collected some of their gear and passed them with his arms full of wet clothing.

The farther John progressed, the less Sarah weighed. Though there was still quite a span between them and the whaler, the water had crept up to his chest and partly set her afloat.

"The tide has come in," remarked Sarah, squirming to keep her foot dry.

"Don't move!" John padded on. The water was squeezing his chest and beginning to lap at his throat and chin. It wasn't far any more. He could make it. He saw Harry climb into the boat, haul up the anchor, start the engine. It tuckered steadily.

Sarah wiggled once more. John floundered and slipped and the water closed above his head. He sank with no surprise. Since he had never learned how to swim, he expected to sink. There was hardly a splash.

❧

At first sight, Thatcher Island always seemed to recover from a fire. Tracts that had looked black and lifeless sprouted green. The birds returned and the air was full of insects. But there was a smaller variety of plants at Gull's Head after a heavy rain washed most of the topsoil off its blackened slopes.

And tall trees were sparse. Some species, like the maple, took a long time in coming back.

At the very moment Harry saw them go under he killed the motor and dived overboard. He did not hesitate. Nor did he stop to think that both Sarah and John were quite capable of saving themselves. Sarah swam better than he did, and John probably was equally competent. The only thing he could think of was that they needed help. A remembered feeling of urgency propelled him to the bottom. Harry skimmed over the sand, grabbed someone's kicking legs and forced a struggling Sarah upwards.

"You idiot, you're drowning me," she sputtered. "It's John."

Harry dove down again. He found John floating and as he shouldered him upward he was at ease in spite of John's weight. His legs pushed deftly. Nothing pulled him down now. He left John clinging to the whaler and rounded the boat. He could have swum for hours and hours. It seemed to him that some burden had been lifted. He was free.

"OK?" Panting, the three grinned at each other in the boat.

Harry turned the engine on and steered the whaler away from the island.

"Is it your wound?" asked Sarah gently. "It's bleeding again, is it? We forgot all about it."

"I can't swim," said John. "I don't have a wound. I

made it up so I wouldn't have to go into the water. You want to look?" Without waiting for her answer he pulled his pants leg up and ripped off the row of Band-Aids. The skin beneath them was smooth.

"You mean you haven't been knifed?" Sarah was clearly disappointed.

"No."

"You should have told us you couldn't swim. We would have made you wear a life preserver all the time. Put it on now!" she admonished him, and John did not catch her laughing at him. "Harry doesn't like the water much either. Since he almost drowned saving someone who wasn't there."

"This time there was," John said.

"Stupid! It wasn't deep enough for that. You would have reached bottom with your head sticking way out. I'll teach you how to swim if you'll fix up my tree house."

They shook hands.

John smiled at Sarah. He was glad he had told her. It made life so much easier for the rest of his stay. Besides, he was sure he would learn quickly. He liked the water and he hadn't been scared floating. He looked over at Harry. They were even. Harry had done everything to save him. And earlier at the pit he had come to Harry's side and leaped down to free Doug Morrison in his place, when Harry couldn't act. They were even.

Harry saw them talking together as the motor howled and he took the whaler out to sea. A broad streamer of smoke rose above the middle of the island, visible for miles and miles. With the wind from the south, the fire was going to eat its way straight toward the sweet-water swamp. Chances were good that it could be halted before sweeping to Baker's Point if help arrived soon. Harry sighed with relief and held direct course to the Egham harbor and the nearest telephone.

"Why isn't anybody here yet?"' Sarah shouted over to him.

"Gifford's Cove is much closer to town." He had thought of it only now. That's why the sea was empty.

Sarah and John kept their eyes on Thatcher Island. It wasn't the same island they had approached just a few hours ago, when they had shivered as if a sudden cold had come up. Despite the smoke welling up from its center, it appeared innocent, with the soft curve of the eastern cove, the sand, the bushy brown-and-green-dotted height and the opal water touching it.

It was a beautiful island, exactly right for a picnic.

"How long ago do you think we came?" asked John.

Sarah didn't bother to study the sun. "Ages," she said.

As Harry skirted Gull's Head they saw a lot of movement in and around the western cove. Boats were landing, their passengers debarking on the beach. Others were being piloted into the cove, dropping sails, anchoring, lowering smaller craft. Equipment was unloaded. It was a busy scene and they were well away from it, since

Harry was heading in a beeline for Egham. John gestured to him to throttle the motor.

"Turn it off!"

Harry shut it off.

"Three more." Sarah pointed to three spots which grew rapidly into powerful boats and whisked past. "Coast guard from the next town."

"No need to report at the fire station," remarked John.

"Do you think so?" Harry looked at John and Sarah and over to the island. "Do you really think so?"

They nodded gravely.

"But I would like to know everything," said Sarah. "Or some of it." They nestled against the life preservers. The water was quite a bit calmer than it had been in the morning and the boat rocked gently. Seated, they saw the column of smoke fray at the tip in the upside-down bowl of blue sky. That's when Harry told the whole story from the beginning. At times he was glad to be hiding behind his mask of red paint and soot, though he realized as he finished that it had not been like one of his mother's long talks where everything was either bad or good and did not change from one into the other while your back was turned. It wasn't that simple.

What had been wrong with wanting to join a game?

"I came to free you, Sarah," he said, and corrected himself. "No, that's not true. I had to get you out of there so they wouldn't know we were together." He didn't like himself much.

"In the pit," he stammered. "It was awful . . . I didn't know I could do it . . . hit like that . . . and I left him . . ." He broke off. "Would I . . . ?"

They did not help him.

He had to answer it for himself.

They were silent for a long time. Sarah traced the red circle around her mouth and John examined his sneakers.

"It couldn't be the island, could it?" Sarah asked.

Harry and John shook their heads.

"It's me all right," said Harry harshly.

There was another long silence.

"It wasn't you alone." Sarah came to his side. "I lied a little and John lied a lot. He can't swim and his wound was a fake. He was never in a real fight and I bet some-one hit him on the back of his head with a can of pine-apple juice by accident."

"V-8." John set her right. "And I didn't want to come here."

"You didn't want to come here?" Sarah and Harry perked up, grateful to tackle another problem. "Why not?"

"I like mountains better," stuttered John. He didn't want to hurt them and he wasn't going to explain how much he hated being pushed on some strange family for free. "On account of how dumb I am in the water." They laughed, though they knew it was not the truth— or only part of it. If that was the way John wanted it, they were going to accept it. Perhaps later he would change his story.

"Look at the fire!"

They leaped up, and as they watched, the banner of smoke dwindled, became flimsy and transparent, and vanished shortly afterwards. Occasional puffs of gray appeared and dissolved. Then they too ceased to rise. Thatcher Island rested serene on the water.

"It's all over." Sarah turned away from the island, her eyes bright. "We got away, didn't we?"

"Sort of," said Harry, lost in thought.

"It's all over?" asked John. "What about your parents?"

"We'll figure out something."

John was sure they would.

"You want to take the whaler back in?" asked Harry. "It won't matter now."

Sarah nodded, delighted.

So with Sarah and John at the controls they roared toward Egham harbor in fancy loops and hair-raising turns which didn't scare Harry. He kept his eyes on Thatcher Island.

The next time he came back to it he would know a lot more.

❧

Thatcher Island was three miles long and a mile

wide, more or less. It floated in the ocean not far from the entrance to Salt Meadow Bay like an enormous seal, its head lifted above the water as if guarding against surprise. Old Mrs. Thatcher had finally made up her mind about its future. There were signs all along the shoreline saying:

WILDLIFE PRESERVE

KEEP OFF!

ABOUT THE AUTHOR

T. DEGENS grew up in eastern Germany. She studied biology in Bonn, immigrated to the United States in 1956, and lived for many years in Falmouth, Massachusetts. At present, Ms. Degens is in Germany with her family, studying psychology at the University of Hamburg in preparation for work with retarded people.

T. Degens is the author of *Transport 7-41-R*, a highly acclaimed first novel that received the first IRA Children's Book Award and the *Boston Globe-Horn Book* Award. She is currently at work on a third novel.